A CHRISTMAS MOON

Evie Price is determined to find her brother Phelan, who went away years before with the wolf men, leaving her family heartbroken. She enlists the help of the enigmatic Professor Raphael. As they travel into a dark and hostile landscape, meeting peoples she has only read about in books, Evie's instincts play tricks on her, leaving her uncertain whether she can trust Raphael. But can he trust himself with someone as precious as Evie?

SALLY QUILFORD

◆

A CHRISTMAS MOON

Complete and Unabridged

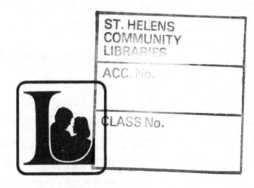

LINFORD
Leicester

First published in Great Britain in 2012

First Linford Edition
published 2016

A catalogue record for this book is available
from the British Library.

ISBN 978–1–4448–3093–4

Published by
F. A. Thorpe (Publishing)
Anstey, Leicestershire

Set by Words & Graphics Ltd.
Anstey, Leicestershire
Printed and bound in Great Britain by
T. J. International Ltd., Padstow, Cornwall

This book is printed on acid-free paper

1

Six-year-old Evie Price awoke when she heard the latch lift on the back door. She slipped out of bed, hesitating only when her tiny feet touched the cold, hard floorboards. Outside, a heavy frost had descended over the land. Momentarily she considered that it might be better to stay in the warmth of her bed, but her eagerness to follow Phelan overruled her dislike of the cold. She went to the window and saw the small form of her brother running across the lawn.

The full moon lighting the icy land-scape in a silvery glow told her exactly where Phelan was going. He was going to look for the wolf men. She stamped her foot, even though there was no one to see her sudden fit of pique. It was not fair that he left her behind! She wanted to see the wolf men too.

'They meet in the forest and drink warm blood from cattle,' their maid, Polly, had said in the kitchen that morning, her eyes gleaming with excitement as she kneaded the dough. 'Some say they're very handsome in human form, but once they turn into beasts . . . ' Despite Polly's ominous tones, she looked even more excited. Evie was too young to understand why at that time, but when she thought back to that moment, many years later, she began to understand Polly's reaction.

'That is quite enough, Polly,' Evie's mother, Harriet, chided weakly. 'You will give Evangeline nightmares. And if the reverend finds out . . . ' Harriet's face held a trace of fear.

'Oh no, Mama,' Evie said, chewing on a piece of warm gingerbread, 'I want to know about the wolf men. Do tell me, Polly.'

'Do *not* tell her, Polly.' Harriet Price's unusually firm tones ended the conversation. Normally no one paid much heed to Harriet. It was the

Reverend Price who ruled the roost at the vicarage, but his wife's fear of his disapproval had overridden her normal frailty.

Later that day Evie found her brother Phelan in deep conversation with Polly, but they stopped when she drew near. Evie's response was one everyone recognised. She burst into tears and had a tantrum, earning a reprimand from her father, who sent her to bed without supper.

'It's not fair,' she had sobbed, beating her pillow so hard that feathers flew into the air. It was not missing supper that bothered her so much, though she had been looking forward to mince pie and custard. No, it was the injustice of it all. Why should Phelan know all about the wolf men when she did not? He was only four years older than her. He was not a grown up, like Mama, Papa and Polly. Oh, it was just too much to bear. She had ranted and railed until exhaustion threw her into a fitful sleep.

Awoken by her brother leaving the house, she crept downstairs, and out through the back door of the vicarage, following as much as she could in her brother's footsteps. She knew her way to the edge of the forest. Only the day before, her friend Tilly had dared her to walk into it. Evie had refused. 'I am not afraid,' she had said haughtily. 'But Mama has told me I must not spoil my dress before Church. Papa expects us to set a good example when he reads his sermons.'

The forest, which descended from light sparse trees to thick dark under-growth very quickly, even in the daylight, looked more foreboding in the dark. 'I am not afraid,' she said to herself, clenching her little fists. She spun around. Was that laughter she heard?

She had no idea where in the forest Phelan and the wolf men might be, so she just scrambled into the under-growth, hoping to find her brother soon. The bright moon helped a little, lighting up a rough pathway to the centre of the forest; but where the thicket was at its most dense, it tore at her clothes and scratched her arms and legs.

What she saw when she found them was most disappointing. Yes, there were men there — sitting around, drinking — but they were just men, not wolves. She looked up at the moon. It was definitely full. They looked no different to the young men who sometimes sat in the market square, drinking from flagons of cider. It was a problem that her father had brought up in several parish council meetings.

'Unfortunately,' he had told the family over dinner one night, 'I am up against apathy and parents who make excuses for their children about there being no jobs or prospects for young men nowadays.'

There was a snapping sound nearby and Evie saw her brother stumble into the clearing.

'Well, well,' said one of the men,

whom Evie recognised as Dolph Lyell, the son of a local landowner, 'if it isn't Phelan, the little wolf.' Dolph stood up, towering over Phelan.

'I want to join you,' said Phelan.

'No. Come back when you're older,' said Dolph. 'This is not a child's game.' There was something strange about him. Evie and Phelan liked to play statues, and she was reminded of that game in the way Dolph stood. He was completely still. Evie was afraid that if he moved very quickly, something awful would be unleashed, but she did not know what.

'Please, Mr. Lyell, I want to be a wolf man.'

'Do you, now? Well, you're a little too young to learn to control your impulses, and it's something we insist on. After all, you don't want to suddenly become like this and not know what to do about it, do you?'

With those words, an amazing, terrifying thing happened. When Evie dreamed of that night in the years that followed, she could have sworn he became a wolf man right in front of her eyes. His features began to change. His body seemed to grow more hair and he appeared to grow in stature. His shirt strained against his chest, and his face contracted into a snarl. 'Go home!' he roared.

Evie screamed and made eye contact with Dolph . . . the wolf man. She was not sure, because everything happened so fast, but he seemed to smile triumphantly. He fell on all fours and started to move towards her.

Before he reached her, Evie felt a big arm clutch her around the waist, and realised that Phelan was under the same man's other arm.

She seemed to have lost the power of speech. She could not even scream again. Terror gripped her. Was this another wolf man, planning to steal her away from Mama and Papa? She wished she had never left her warm bed. She wished stupid Polly and stupid Phelan had never mentioned the wolf men. She wished Mama was there, holding her, telling her that everything would be alright. She would not mind if her Papa scolded her — as he often did nowadays, because she found it so hard to be a good girl like he wanted her to be — as long as she was safe and warm at home.

'Put me down!' she finally managed to say, her arms flailing as she tried to strike him. It made no difference: she was too weak, and he was incredibly strong.

'Be quiet, child!' he said in a gruff voice. 'If you want to live, for God's sake be quiet.'

'You must not take the Lord's name in vain,' Evie said, shocked to the core. What would Papa say?

'The Lord forsook me a long time ago. He does not hear my prayers, so He is hardly going to hear my curses.'

They had reached the vicarage gate. The man put Evie and Phelan on their feet. They both had trouble standing, their legs were trembling so much. 'Go inside and don't come out on a full moon again. Do you hear?'

'You can't tell me what to do,' said Phelan. 'I want to be a wolf man.'

'Then you're a damn fool.'

'I'm going to tell Papa on you for swearing,' said Evie. Rather than being afraid, the man laughed. She could not see his face clearly as the moon was behind him. But his laughter infuriated her. 'You're a bad man and you'll go straight to Hell.'

She felt, rather than saw, him stiffen. 'And you, little one,' he said in a cold hard voice, bending down so he was face to face with her, still leaving his own features in shadow, 'need to learn to control your temper. Otherwise it will be the undoing of you.'

Evie answered by kicking him in the shins. His laughter followed her all the way up the garden path.

★ ★ ★

The night in the forest haunted Evie for many years, to the point that, as she matured and was able to think it through more rationally, she was able to convince herself that it had all just been a bad dream. Her parents had sent her to bed without any supper, and she had simply turned her anger and Polly's mention of the wolf men into a dark fantasy, during which she had never left her bed. There was comfort in that thought, even if somewhere at the back of her mind she knew she was fooling herself.

Phelan never spoke of it, which increased her conviction that it could not have really happened. But as the years went on, and her brother passed through puberty, he became more brooding. Her parents talked in hush tones about the sullen, morose creature their son had become.

The wolf men, Polly told them not long after that night in the forest, had left the area. One evening eleven years later, with another full moon due, she happily informed them that the wolf men had returned.

'Farmer Hooper said he saw them last full moon, heading back to the forest. I bet they'll be there tonight an' all,' Polly said as she put a mince pie in the oven. The very aroma of the pies, filling the kitchen with sweet, spicy goodness, brought that earlier night back into seventeen-year-old Evie's mind. Poring over her books, she tried to push it aside, but it would not leave her.

She waited for her mother to chastise Polly, but Harriet Price, like her son, had become increasingly morose as time went on. Once or twice Evie had overheard her mother and father mid-conversation.

'It will be soon,' Harriet would say.

'It is a superstition, Harriet; nothing more, nothing less. Really, dearest, I did hope that once we married, these wild fantasies of yours would abate. You promised you would be a sensible and loving wife.'

'Sensible, yes,' Harriet had said, coldly. 'But it is hard to show love to a man who gives no love in return. And that same fate awaits . . . '

Reverend Price had coughed, to let Evie know that he was aware of her presence out in the hallway. 'It is all nonsense, Harriet,' he said. 'Your mother believed the old legends far too much. Such superstitions are ridiculous.'

Evie did not move away. The conversation was too interesting.

'Not the same as believing a man died and was resurrected three days later,' Harriet had snapped.

'Enough! You will not mock the Lord in such a way in my presence.' Evie heard a book being slammed shut. 'Really, Harriet, it's bad enough that Polly fills our children's heads with such idiotic thoughts. It can be expected of a servant. Believe me, if she were not so good at her job and it not so difficult to replace her on what I am able to pay, I should have dismissed her years ago. I had hoped you would set a better example. Evie was almost feral as a child, and Phelan . . . Phelan becomes worse every day. Sometimes I can hardly believe I married a woman of such . . . '

'Passion,' Harriet had said. 'Passion is the word you're looking for, Charles. What a pity you never manage to find it. Perhaps if my life had had some sense of romance and passion in it, I would not fall back on what you call wild fantasies.'

Realising that she really should not be listening to this part of the conversation, Evie had escaped upstairs to her room.

Now, looking at her mother across the kitchen table, as Polly chatted away about the wolf men, she began to realise for the first time that Harriet had never been a happy woman. She had been a loving mother, but not a very stern one. Discipline had been left to Reverend Price.

Odd, thought Evie, how even she thought of her father as Reverend Price. She had perhaps heard his Christian name three or four times in her life, as her mother also referred to him as Reverend Price, or 'your father' when addressing the children. Though Evie addressed him as Papa, he might just as well have been a stranger who just happened to lodge in the same house as them. He had never hugged her, or given her a goodnight kiss. He had once patted her on the head, but immediately hesitated, and instead acted as if he was looking for something he had lost, rather than making affectionate contact with his daughter.

Her mother must have also craved affection from her husband, only to be met with cold civility.

'Are you unwell, Mama?' asked Evie over the kitchen table. 'You look pale.'

'I am a little tired, that is all, Evangeline. I think I will go to bed early tonight. Will you sit with Papa at supper? You know how he hates it when I am not there.'

It was a rule that no one dared break. Supper was served at seven o'clock on the dot, and one either had to be away on a trip or very sick indeed in order not to attend the evening meal with the reverend.

'Of course.'

Several hours later, Evie lay in her bed; and, just as she had eleven years before, she heard the back door close. Had she been listening for it? Yes, she rather thought she had.

Phelan had been morose all through supper. Her father had been somewhere in a world of his own, so Evie wondered whether he would even have noticed if no one attended the meal. But Phelan kept watching first the clock, then the sky outside, to the point that, even during his own reverie, their father got up and closed the curtains in one violent movement.

Phelan was going to the wolf men again. Evie knew it. Almost without wanting to, she got out of bed, and put her clothes on. She had to go too. She had to find out whether her nightmares had been real or imagined. Once she laid the ghost to rest, she would be able to sleep at night. And perhaps, she hoped, if Phelan also realised it was just a silly fantasy, he might be happier too. He could go away to college or join the army, instead of sitting in the vicarage brooding about a life that, even if it existed, would only bring him misery.

With a distinct feeling of déjà vu, Evie ran through the grass to the edge of the forest. As she did so, that first night came back to her. She even remembered Tilly's dare. The full moon seemed to accentuate all her emotions, all her memories, almost as if it fed from them, bringing them to the fore and making her feel more alive than she had ever felt. No, that was not true. The last time she had felt so alive was back then, when the fear and excitement had been almost unbearable. Yet she had to admit, she missed it when it was gone after she settled back into her normal childhood life. She even half-understood why Phelan wanted to be with the wolf men. Her brief glimpse of them had shown a world which few people entered. It was a world of mystery and excitement, a world of living outside society's rules.

But . . . she slowed down a little as the thought took hold . . . where would that mystery and excitement lead? *Straight to the gates of Hell*, an inner voice whispered. Half-remembered gossip from Polly filled her head. That wolf men were damned for eternity, unless they redeemed themselves somehow. More than anything, she had to save Phelan from his own recklessness. She would reason with him, beg him to come home. Her father's austere teachings had instilled in her the fear of the fires of Hell, both for herself and for her loved ones. She could not bear to think of her brother being damned for all eternity.

'Phelan . . . ' she whispered, quickening her step again.

She reached the same clearing in the woods and saw the same group of men sitting on logs, drinking spirits from pewter jugs. It was not just that the men were the same. They had not changed at all. They should have looked ten years older but they did not. Even Dolph still looked like a man in his mid-twenties, when Evie was sure that he should be in his thirties by now.

'I want to join you,' she heard a voice say. It was her brother.

'Well, look who is all grown up,' said Dolph, grinning and taking a drink. 'Are you sure you're ready for this, little wolf?'

'I've been ready forever.'

'So you're ready to be chased out of every town you enter. You're ready to have people spit at you in the street. Are you ready to be damned for all eternity?'

'I only exist as I am now,' said Phelan. 'I want to be alive. To feel the things you do. To experience the things you do. I'm twenty-one years old. I'm old enough to make the choice now.'

'Very well . . . ' Dolph put down his flagon of ale and stood up, stretching his arms to the moonlight.

Evie wanted to cry out, but terror gripped her throat as Dolph growled and moved towards Phelan. 'No! Phelan!' she managed to croak out in a tiny voice. Dolph should not have heard her, but he did. As his mouth moved towards Phelan's neck, but in such a way Evie could not see the actual bite, his head turned and his eyes locked on hers.

Her brother fell to the floor, with a wide smile on his face. He had got what he wanted, but Dolph was no longer interested in Phelan. He was moving with immense speed towards Evie.

She turned and began to run; and, just as she had eleven years before, she felt herself lifted from the ground. The man holding her spun around — was he a man? Or was he a wolf like Dolph? She did not know, but she felt the animal in him come to life, and the veins pulsating in his arms. 'Not her . . . ' he said to Dolph. 'Leave her alone.'

Dolph faltered a little. How could he

be afraid of the man holding her? He was a monster, and the man was . . . what, exactly? She felt that she had become an intrinsic part of something she did not understand.

The man and the wolf man glared at each other in the night, and she could hear laboured breath coming from them both. 'You know what happens if you take me on,' said the man holding Evie. 'I don't think you want that. I'm willing to take it to the final conclusion, Dolph. Are you?'

She did not know if she imagined it, but the wolf . . . Dolph . . . seemed to laugh, then turn back.

'No, I didn't think so,' the man muttered. He ran through the trees, still with Evie in his arms.

'I think I can walk now,' she said.
'Excuse me?'
'Be quiet. I'm not putting you down until I know you're safe.'

Once again he took her to the gate of the vicarage, deftly lifting her over it, before dropping her on the ground. 'If you take my advice,' he said, 'you'll never leave this garden. You're safe here, little girl. Stay that way.' She still could not make out his face, to see if he was man or wolf. He always stood with his back to the moon, casting himself in shadow.

'What about my brother? What will happen to him? We must save him.'

'Phelan is never coming home. He's lost to you, and all that is good and pure in the world.' The man started to walk away, and then turned back. 'Remember, when the events of this night eat you up inside, that your brother chose his path. Some don't get to choose.'

2

The offices of *The Full Moon Gazette* bustled with activity, and even a year after starting her job as a reporter, Evie had that familiar sense of excitement when she entered them. Men smoking pipes sat huddled over typewriters, clacking away with one finger in order to get their copy in on time.

There was only one other woman, the wife of the local lord. It was her job to deal with the popular agony aunt column. What most readers did not realise was that the majority of problems were made up, and a way for her ladyship to instil her own values on feckless womanhood. If you wanted to know how to deal with fractious servants, she had the answer. She could tell you where to sit a Rear Admiral at a dinner party. But if any young girl without servants — or a dining table at which to seat a Rear Admiral — dared to write in a real letter about a real problem with a real man, her ladyship's only answer to any problem regarding matters of the heart was simply: 'Do not do it'. Do not fall in love with the wrong man. Do not even fall in love with the right man.

'After all,' her ladyship had confided in Evie, 'what do common people really know of love? If you ask me, it is merely an excuse amongst the lower classes to commit sin and breed. It is much better if they avoid it altogether.'

Evie did not know whether to be pleased or offended that Her Ladyship seemed to count her as an equal. She sometimes wished she could reply to the young women involved and give them some useful advice.

Her Ladyship looked up and smiled benignly as Evie passed by on her way to the editor's office. 'Do not forget to tell the dear reverend that we expect you both at dinner on Friday night,' she said.

'Papa is very much looking forward to it,' said Evie. It was a diplomatic version of her father's response to the invitation.

'My nephew Herbert will be there. He is such a nice young man. Yet, he is finding it impossible to meet a nice girl with whom to settle down. I hate to say it, dear child, but you are not getting any younger. What are you now? Twenty-seven? I wonder at your father letting you turn into an old maid, really I do. But thankfully Herbert is not too fussy . . . '

Evie smiled and rushed past, not wanting to hear anything else about young Herbert. She had met him once, and that was enough to convince her that being an old maid was much preferable to marrying a chinless wonder who had no real calling in the world. He might not be fussy, but she certainly was. She would much rather marry a poor but hard-working man than someone who was content to live off his rich relatives.

'Ah, there you are, Miss Price,' said Mr. Marr, the editor, when she entered his office. He beckoned for her to shut the door. 'I see you managed to escape Her Ladyship's attempts at matchmaking. She caught me earlier, telling me that six months is quite long enough to grieve my late wife, and that she has a nice middle-aged cousin . . . '

'Oh, I'm so sorry,' said Evie. 'That was awful of her.'

'I think I'd be less forgiving if she realised she was doing it. I honestly think she means well in her way. I've told her that I'm not ready to replace Cissy just yet. If ever . . . ' He fell into a reverie, which was something he had done a lot lately. Evie almost felt guilty for taking advantage of it, but felt she had no choice. She took the seat opposite him.

'Mr. Marr; you know, I suppose, that there's a full moon on Christmas Day this year.'

'So I'd heard . . . the last six times you told me.' His face changed from morose to a wide grin.

'And you also know I've been studying werewolves . . . '

'Yes, you told me that too.'

'I've heard from someone at the Hungarian embassy that there's a man living in that country who hunts them. His name is Professor Raphael. What I wondered was, whether you would be interested in an interview with him about his work.'

'You want the newspaper to pay for a trip to Hungary?'

'No, no, I can do that myself. Unless you wanted to fund the trip, of course,' she said with a hopeful smile. 'What I really need is the time off to go. I have several articles finished, so I won't be leaving you high and dry.'

'I'd be happy to let you go, Miss Price, but will your father permit it?'

'I've already worked that out, don't worry.'

'Miss Price . . . Evie . . . you must know how fond we all are of you. I've known you since you were a little girl. A very bad-tempered little girl, if I remember rightly.' He smiled again. Evie blushed, remembering what a horror she had been back then. 'But there's always been good in you. We can all see that. That was why I gave you a chance with the newspaper. I also know about what happened to your brother. Or what was supposed to have happened. Wolf men and all that.'

'I have heard that our maid Polly is your best informant in the area,' said Evie, wryly.

'Oh, she's a wonderful source of largely useless information. Surely you don't believe in all that nonsense? I know you write about myths and legends. Your column is very popular. But I've always thought of you as a level-headed sort of girl, despite your interest in supernatural matters. I don't want you to go off on some wild goose chase to talk to a man who is clearly a charlatan. He may be a charlatan who's managed to con a large number of the European nobility, but he's still a quack when all's said and done. There are no wolf men, Evie. There are no vampires, no shapeshifters, and no ghosts.'

She smiled. 'I wonder why you allow my column!'

'It keeps the readers happy. They love that sort of stuff, just as hopeless young women love being told what to do by a real live Lady. My job is to sell papers, regardless of what rubbish is between the pages. But it's one thing to write about it speculatively. What you intend to do is interview a man who wants to convince people there is some value in his work.'

'Mr. Marr, I'll be honest with you. What I really want to do is find my brother, and I think the Professor can lead me to him. Some friends travelling in Hungary saw Phelan in the area recently. I need the cover of my post here in order to talk to this man.'

'Then you must go, if that is your real reason. I know how much sadness Phelan's loss has caused your family. Perhaps you can bring it all to an end.

However, do try and keep your feet on the ground, Evie. Come back to us safely. And do not let this charlatan Raphael cause you more pain and suffering.'

'Thank you.'

Convincing Mr. Marr was the easy part. Bringing her father around to her way of thinking proved to be harder.

'Mr. Marr told me all about it,' he told Evie over dinner. 'And I am glad he did, before you go wasting our money on this Raphael fellow.'

'*My* money, Papa,' said Evie. Her aunt had died recently, leaving Evie a lump sum and a small annuity. 'And if I wish to spend it finding Phelan, then I will. We promised Mama . . . '

The reverend fell into silence for a long time, picking at the food on his plate. When he eventually spoke, it was with quiet fury. 'I do not need you to remind me of the promise we made to your mother on her deathbed. But I also promised to love and protect you.'

'Papa, I am twenty-seven years old. I

29

have managed, so far, to take care of myself.'

'No, Evangeline, I have managed to take care of you. And that has not been easy, given your flighty nature.'

'I am not flighty,' said Evie, her own anger rising. 'To say such a thing suggests that I am immoral.'

'I did not mean it that way,' said the reverend, holding up his hand. 'I apologise. I know that you are a good girl underneath all that energy and anger. Lady Bedlington called on me today . . . '

'The answer is no,' said Evie. 'I am not interested in Herbert.'

'Yes, that is very much what I told her. And I do not blame you. He is a rather useless young man. But do you not wish to marry at some time, Evangeline? I am not getting any younger and it would be nice to have grandchildren sitting on my knee.'

'Strange,' said Evie, 'but I do not remember ever sitting on your knee as a child.'

'I . . . ' The reverend looked lost for words. 'I realise I have failed you in many ways, child. This is why I try so hard to protect you now. I am afraid that you believe all this nonsense about the wolf men. Phelan certainly believed it, and we lost him. I do not wish to lose you too.'

Evie did something she had never done before. She reached out and put her hand over her father's. 'I have no wish to join them, Papa. I merely want to bring Phelan home, where he belongs. Besides, I have been researching werewolves. I do not really believe Phelan became a wolf man, but there is a mental condition called lycanthropy whereby people believe they have become werewolves. I think that this is the key to Phelan's problem. If we could bring him home, and get him the proper treatment . . . '

'And you say this condition really exists?' asked the reverend thoughtfully.

'Yes. There are documented cases, written up by respected physicians. I can show them to you. Phelan wanted it so much as a child that I am certain he believes that he has become a were-wolf.'

Evie only half-lied to her father. The idea of mental illness was one explanation for what she had seen in the forest so many years earlier. She also had her own ideas. Sometimes she dismissed those ideas as ridiculous. Such a thing was not possible at the dawn of the twentieth century. Other times, mostly after a night of fevered dreams, she awoke convinced by what she had seen. Either way, she had to help Phelan.

It often occurred to her that by helping her brother, she would also help herself in some way. Set free from the nightmares and fears which marred her life, she might be able to move on. Perhaps once Phelan was found, she could settle down and marry. Not to Herbert. Anyone but Herbert! Lady Bedlington had not been wrong about Evie getting on in years and becoming an old maid. As often as Evie told herself she did not need a husband to give her life meaning, there were also other times when she sat and imagined what it would be like to love and be loved. To have children sitting on her knee and a man sitting opposite, reading his paper. The longing for that life sometimes became unbearable. After Phelan disappeared, the whole family had moved into what could only be described as limbo. It seemed to her that every conversation for the past eleven years had begun, 'When Phelan comes home . . . '

It was not 'When Christmas is over' or 'When Easter has passed', definite dates by which one could arrange one's life. Plans for the future were always nebulous and based on that vague date when her brother returned. They could not even go on holiday, just in case Phelan came back whilst they were away.

Even Evie's plans to work at the paper were postponed several times. 'We do not know what will happen when Phelan returns,' her mother and father had said. Only after her mother's death did Evie put her foot down with her father and insist she was going to go out to work. She was tired of putting her life on hold. She also had to think of her father and the promise they had made to her mother. It having been instilled in her so often that life could not really begin until Phelan came home, she decided that, rather sit and wait for her brother to return, she would go and fetch him. If he refused to return, it would at least be something definite by which to plan the future. Only then could she begin to live her own life.

'I intend to travel to Hungary at the beginning of December,' she told her father over the dinner table. She had decided earlier that day not to ask his permission. She was over the age of majority, after all.

'Then I intend to travel to Hungary with you,' said the reverend. 'No matter how mature you believe you are,

Evangeline, you are still my daughter and my responsibility.'

Evie's heart dropped, and she finally admitted to herself that part of her plan included escaping from the oppression of her father and the vicarage. 'I am old enough to travel alone,' she insisted.

'Let me be the judge of that. Besides, I have a hankering to visit the Holy Land. So if we do not find Phelan, we will go on there. It will do us both good.'

'Very well, Papa,' said Evie, deciding that she would have to be content with small victories for now. She would be leaving the vicarage and travelling abroad. Her father might be with her, but it was still an adventure!

3

Budapest

'I think this is the place, Papa,' said
Evie. She looked at the scrap of paper
in her hand, then up at the imposing
gothic building. Snow-covered gar-
goyles stared down from the roof, and
Evie fancied for a moment she saw one
move, but put it down to nerves and
hunger. They had only arrived by train
an hour before and had not had time to
find somewhere to eat. 'The name is on
the plate. *Professor Raphael. Fourth
floor.*'

If anything, the building was even
colder inside. A large marble hall
offered only a modicum of heat from an
inglenook fireplace. They could see
their breath rising in mist as they
climbed the staircase.

'Do you really think this man will

help us to find him, Evangeline?' Reverend Price asked.

'The man at the embassy said that Professor Raphael is the foremost expert on myths and legends.'

'Myths and legends, yes. But how is that going to help us to find Phelan? I know what you believe, and I know what your mother believed . . . ' The reverend paused on the stairs. Evie suspected it was as much to get his breath as to deal with the anguish her mother's death had caused him.

When Phelan disappeared, an investigation learned he had been seen leaving the area with a group of men. As there had been no suspicion that he had been taken against his own free will, and because he was over the age of majority, the case was closed as far as the authorities were concerned. Harriet Price became a shadow, haunting the vicarage, finally dying at the turn of the century.

Before she died, with Evie and the reverend at her bedside, she had made her husband promise to bring Phelan home.

'You must forgive him, Charles,' she had said. 'It is the only way his soul may be saved.'

'Forgive him?' her father had said savagely. 'He has destroyed this family with his actions.'

'Poor Charles,' Harriet had said, 'the idea of unconditional love always escaped you, didn't it? Along with the Christian charity you preach so much about. I wish you could have loved me.'

'It goes without saying that I did,' said the reverend, glancing uncomfortably at his daughter.

'No, Charles. It does not go without saying. A woman needs to hear it.' Her mother had gone quiet, and they thought she had fallen asleep, until her eyes opened and she stared at her husband in anguish. 'Please, you must promise me that you'll bring Phelan home.'

'I will find out where he is, and ask him if he wants to return.'

'That is all I can hope for.' Harriet took a deep breath. It was to be one of her last. 'One more thing, Charles . . . '

'What is it, Harriet?'

'No matter what happens, you must love Evangeline. Even if Phelan chose his path, she did not choose hers.'

Harriet died a few moments later, leaving Evie wondering what her mother meant. When she tried to ask her father, he brushed her away. 'It is nothing. Just an idle fancy of your mother's. She was a good woman, but she had too many of those fantasies. Like all this rubbish about Phelan joining the wolf men. It's all silly, Dark Ages superstition.'

It was therefore no small miracle that her father had accompanied her to Europe to see Professor Raphael. Since her mother's death, he had become almost hermit-like. She could see him fading just as she had seen her mother do the same. What was more, Evie had also become isolated, caring as she did for her father all the time. If she had not left the vicarage, she thought she might go insane looking at the same drab four walls daily.

It said a lot about how her father's spirit had sunk that once the decision to leave was made, he allowed himself to be organised by the daughter he had spent so many years trying to tame. 'You're a good girl, Evangeline,' he had said during their long journey. 'I was afraid when you were younger that we might have more trouble with you. What a pity I did not take as much notice of Phelan's sullen nature as I did of your fiery one. It's that red hair, of course. All the Pendragon women have it. Your mother's hair was the colour of hot coals when we first met . . . ' He drifted into the past, which was something he had done a lot since Harriet died. It gave Evie brief glimpses into his life with her mother that, as a child growing up with their cold civility, she had never seen.

'Come along, Papa,' she said as they

climbed the stairs to Professor Raphael's office. 'The sooner we speak to the Professor, the sooner we can find somewhere to stay the night.'

For some reason, Evie had expected an elderly, grey-haired man, surrounded by dusty books. The Professor's office was certainly full of those, along with maps and charts of all kinds — including one charting the lunar cycle, which was pinned on the wall. She noted, with interest, that he had marked Christmas Day as the date of the next full moon.

A large desk stood in the middle of the room, and around it were easy chairs and a couple of sofas. She did not know for certain, but she suspected that one of the sofas had been recently slept upon. She went as far as to guess the owner slept on it continually. All this she was able to take in before someone entered from a side room, wiping his hands on a towel.

The man who appeared was no old and musty Professor. He was tall. Huge, in fact. Well over six feet tall, and with strong, broad, shoulders. His hair was a thick, dark mass of unruly curls, longer than the norm; and he had a dark beard, which he at least seemed to keep trim. But it was his eyes that tore into Evie's soul. They were a piercing blue colour, fringed by dark lashes, below thick eyebrows. She had the feeling that she knew those eyes, or at least the force of them upon her, but could not remember ever having met him. His age was hard to define. He looked to be in his mid- to late-thirties, and yet there was some air of an old soul about him.

'Professor Raphael?' she said when she was able to speak. She held out her hand in a business-like fashion, but withdrew it under the force of that gaze. Alright, so he did not want to shake her hand. That was not unusual. Some old-fashioned men had problems with a strong woman. 'You are Professor Raphael, are you not? My name is Evie Price. This is my father, Reverend Price. I sent you a note a week ago. I work for *The Full Moon Gazette*, and am interested in learning about local myths and legends. I am reliably informed that you are the man to help me.'

Professor Raphael did not speak. He just continued to look at her.

'Would you mind if my father sat down?' Evie said, faltering under that terrifying gaze. 'He is very tired, and . . . ' Raphael indicated a sofa at the side of the room, which the reverend gratefully took.

'I do not give interviews to newspapers,' Raphael said at last. 'And neither do I help little girls pretending to be journalists.' His accent was hard to pin down. She would have said he was English, but the edges had blurred on the cut-glass vowels, giving him a slight transatlantic drawl. She gleaned from that he had also spent some time in America.

'I assure you that I do not pretend, Professor Raphael,' said Evie, breathing deeply, trying to stem her growing temper. What an infuriating man! She had imagined that someone described as a charlatan would have more charm, and also be willing to pretend interest in what she had to say.

'No, that is why you are writing about myths and legends instead of covering parliamentary issues. Tell me, Miss Price, do you write the horoscopes too? Promising plain, uneducated women that the tall, dark, handsome man of their dreams is waiting just around the corner?'

'It seems hardly fitting for you to mock me when you spend your whole life surrounded by myths and legends, Professor Raphael.'

'My aim is to dispense with them once and for all. I want to shine a light into dark corners. I don't write fantastical stories about vampires and werewolves in order to thrill an excitable public.'

Reverend Price spoke. 'I am very heartened to hear you say that, Professor Raphael.' He stood up and walked over to the Professor, his feet still a little unsteady. 'I too hate all these superstitions, and I am sure my daughter does not really believe them either.' The reverend took a deep breath. 'I will be honest with you, Professor Raphael. We are not here because my daughter wishes to write an article for her newspaper. Many years ago my son went missing, apparently travelling with . . . wolf men.'

'Werewolves, you mean.'

'Yes, yes, if you wish to call them that.'

'We are told,' said Evie, more than a little annoyed that Professor Raphael seemed to be taking her father more seriously than her, 'that there is a mental condition called lycanthropy. Where men are convinced they are werewolves, and live their lives accordingly. We believe that my brother is suffering from this condition. Some friends of ours who were travelling in this area saw him recently. So we would be grateful for anything that you could tell us about their . . . habits . . . the way they live . . . where they live . . . anything that might help us to find him and bring him home.'

'And subject him to hot and cold baths, electric shock treatment . . . '

'No!' Evie's eyes widened in horror. 'No, of course not.'

'Then how else do you hope to save him from this condition? Men who believe they are wolves are not so easily persuaded otherwise.'

'We just thought that if he saw us . . . if he knew that we loved him and that he could come home, then he would be alright again.'

Raphael smiled, and it was something quite spectacular, lighting up his whole face, making him seem younger. 'It's a nice thought, Miss Price, that love conquers all. I'm sure it's something you tell your readers all the time. And I'm sure that, because of that pretty face of yours, some of them believe you . . . '

'Professor Raphael, I have no idea

what happened in your life to turn you into such a misogynist, and such a cynic . . . '

'Evangeline!' Her father's stern tones told her that once again she had gone too far. Why was it perfectly acceptable for Raphael to mock her, but not for her to stick up for herself? It was not fair . . . She reined in her temper, remembering the many nights as a child when she had muttered those same words into her pillow. She had promised herself she would stop thinking life was unfair, and simply go out and make sure it was fair. It was not easy, however, when women were still shackled by social expectations.

'Reverend Price,' said Raphael, 'I have always believed honesty is the best policy. In which case, I will be honest with you. Go home, and take your pretty daughter with you. You are wasting your time here. Your son is lost to you.'

'Thank you for your honesty, Professor Raphael. We shall not bother you further. Come along, Evangeline.'

Your son is lost to you ... Your brother is lost to you.

The words beat like a tattoo in Evie's head as she walked back down the stairs with her father. They had almost reached the bottom when she said, 'Papa, I think I left my notebook upstairs.'

'We will go back and fetch it.'

'No, the stairs are too much for you. Look, there is a seat over there. Rest a moment. I will only be a couple of minutes.'

She took the stairs two at a time and made her way to Raphael's room, but flew straight into him in the corridor. He held her arms in a strong grip.

'You were there!' she said, accusingly. 'The night Phelan went with Dolph and the others. You were there. You were going to fight Dolph.'

He neither admitted nor denied her accusation. 'It was very clever of you to find out about lycanthropy. Was that the only way you could convince your father to come?'

Evie did not bother to tell Raphael that her main problem had been trying to put her father off travelling with her. 'He does not believe in werewolves, so I had to convince him that my brother had the mental condition. But you do believe, because you were there. So why won't you help us?'

'I told you then, Evie, and I'm telling you now, your brother is lost to you. No amount of Christian charity is going to save him.'

'So you remember me . . . '

'I remember the nasty kick in the shins you gave me when you were a little girl.' He paused. 'And then all that red hair, flowing in the moonlight, when you were . . . what? Sixteen? Seventeen?' His nostrils flared.

'You saved my life. Twice. Why won't you help us now?'

'Because I may not be able to save your life the next time, and I don't want that responsibility.'

'I can take care of myself, Professor

Raphael, despite your low opinion of women. All I need to know is how to save my brother. There must be a way.'

He held her away from him, but did not loosen his grip on her arms. 'I cannot help you. If I did, then I would be signing your death warrant. I did not save your life twice to take you straight to your death now.'

'Why did you save my life? Surely it means there's some good in you.'

He pulled her closer, roughly this time. His touch excited her far more than it should have. 'Don't ever fool yourself into believing I'm good, Evangeline. Believe I am a misogynist, believe I am cynical. Believe anything, so long as you hate me and stay far away from me. But do not ever believe I am a good man. I will only take you straight to the gates of your destruction, and . . . '

He looked down at her, and then before she knew it, his lips found hers in a wild and hungry kiss that almost knocked her off her feet. She knew she should push him away and slap his face. No man had ever dared be so forward with her before. Yet she wanted that kiss; hungered for it almost as much as he did.

He pulled away, emitting an animal-like growl. 'I cannot help you. I will not help you. Go home, Evie. Find a nice man to marry, have half a dozen red-haired children, and be old and fat and happy. But don't ever come near me again.'

He turned and stormed away from her, leaving her feeling a myriad of emotions. Desire, anger, frustration, even more desire . . . where had that come from? She disliked him, didn't she? But she had never been kissed like that in her entire life, and when he stopped kissing her, it was almost as if he had cut off a limb; as if he was supposed to be a part of her and she were a part of him.

Her emotions about Raphael were further confused by the fact that he had twice saved her life. Surely that meant something? It meant, she realised with growing certainty, that despite his words, he was a man she could trust. Twice, despite her own bad behaviour, he had made sure she was safe. A man like that must have a good side to him. Or perhaps it was just wishful thinking, because of the kiss. How many of her friends had fallen for unkind men, only to insist that those men had some good points — if they could only remember what they were? Sadly, the men had not had enough good points to override the bad points. Not that her friends ever listened, just as she knew she would not listen if someone warned her away from Raphael.

Despite her confused emotions, and never one to back down in a fight, Evie walked back to Raphael's room. She found him standing in the centre, running his hands through his thick hair, and looking as tortured as she felt.

'I told you to go,' he said, glaring at her with animal passion.

'I will go. But I am determined to

find my brother, so if you can't help me, perhaps you can point me towards someone who can.'

'Evie . . . ' His voice became dark and dangerous.

'As I told you, Professor Raphael, I am not your concern. If I ask someone else to help me, you do not need to feel responsibility for anything that may or may not happen to me.'

'Oh, you foolish girl. Dolph will kill you if you get in the way. As long as you're at home, you're safe.'

'Why does Dolph want to kill me?'

'I did not say he wanted to. I said he would.'

'No, that's not true. When you were going to fight him, he wanted to kill me then. And when I was a child. I saw it in his eyes. Why me?'

'It's a long story.'

'And one which you're going to tell me, when I hire you to help me find my brother. Just me. Not my father.'

'Does anyone ever dare say no to you? Perhaps it will be a good lesson to you when I do. I've told you I'm not going to do it.'

'Alright; then I'll find someone else.'

'Damn you! You really are the most infuriating girl I've ever met. You always have been. No matter what I say, you're going to do this, aren't you? Go running off into danger, just as you did when you were a child. You give no thought to the consequences.'

'Yes, that is pretty much what I plan. So you'll help me? Because no matter what you say, I know you'll take care of me, like you did before.'

'Don't be so sure. I still owe you a kick in the shins. I might let Dolph kill you on that score alone.' He grinned wryly.

'No, you won't. Because you're not like that.'

'I've already warned you, don't get any romantic notions about me, Evie.'

It was difficult not to, after that kiss, but Evie made a silent vow not to let Raphael get under her skin again. She had to concentrate on the matter in hand. 'Don't worry. It's strictly business. Does that mean you'll help?'

'Can I just state for the record how much I dislike you for making me feel responsible for you?' He sighed, clearly beaten. 'It seems that destiny is not going to allow me to avoid you, no matter how hard I try.'

It occurred to Evie later that it was an odd thing for him to say.

4

'I needed to speak to you without my father,' Evie said, some hours later. She had changed out of her travelling clothes and wore a long black jacket over a white pouter pigeon blouse, teamed with a long black trumpet skirt. It was the 'uniform' she wore when she performed her duties as a journalist, and she hoped it might make Raphael take her more seriously, though she doubted it.

She sat opposite him in his cluttered office. 'As you know, he is working on the assumption that my brother has the mental condition of lycanthropy. Whilst we search for Phelan, it is best that he labours under that illusion; otherwise, he will call off the search as a fool's errand. So I need you to tell me all I need to know about werewolves.' She tried to sound business-like; yet, beneath her prim clothes, her heart still fluttered. She prayed that Raphael could not see how much he affected her.

'The first thing you need to know,' said Raphael, leaning back in his chair, 'is that lycanthropy applies to both states. The mental affliction and the physical process of turning into a werewolf. So it won't be too difficult to discuss it in front of your father. Be aware that those who have the mental affliction believe that they undergo the same changes as a real werewolf. They are often even capable of the same strength and violence. They are also convinced that they came by the disease because they were bitten.'

'You say it's a disease? Being a real werewolf, I mean.'

'Yes. It's carried through the blood — and often through the bloodline, so that anyone who is afflicted can pass the disease onto their children.' His eyes darkened.

Evie wondered for a moment whether Phelan might have had children in the ensuing years. If so, that was another problem she and her father might have to face. 'So, unless one is born into a family of werewolves, one is only infected when one is bitten?'

'That is only the most common way of spreading the disease. It can also be caused by a curse.'

'You mean from a witch?' Something stirred in Evie's memory. A tale her mother used to tell ... but it was snatched away from her, perhaps because of the personality of the man sitting opposite. It was difficult to think clearly in his company, and she had to stay focused if she wanted to save her brother.

'A very powerful sorcerer. Or sorceress. Even Christian saints have been known to curse others with werewolfery. There are other ways, though many are just legends and have little basis in fact. Some say if you sleep outside on a summer night with the full moon on your face, you will undergo metamorphosis. Another legend says you must drink the rainwater from the footprints of a werewolf. Then there's Satanic allegiance — or the opposite. One self-proclaimed werewolf, many years ago, was convinced that he was the Hound of God, sent to fight Satan and his minions. No one believed him.'

Evie shivered. The idea of anyone choosing that path was hard for her to comprehend. She felt, even sitting in Raphael's office in the middle of a bustling European town, that she was travelling into the depths of something dark and diseased. She feared that somewhere along the line she might lose her own humanity.

'Tell me, if you can, Professor Raphael . . . '

'Call me Raphael. Most people do.'

'Raphael, why would anyone want to become such a creature? It's what Phelan wanted, nearly all his life, but I never really understood it.'

'Some people are drawn to the darkness and violence. In what you might call 'real' life, people drink too much or take opium to escape the drudgery of everyday life. For those drawn to the wolf men, it is something else they seek. Sometimes it's merely the permission to do all the things they are not allowed to do in their human state, due to the laws and morals of society.'

'You've told me twice that Phelan is lost to us. What do you mean by that?'

'A werewolf is damned for all eternity.'

'Is there no means of redemption?'

'There is, but you need not think that your brother will care for redemption after having chosen to become a werewolf.'

'What way? You must tell me.'

'A werewolf *might* be redeemed as long as he does not bite another, though there is no assurance of it. It goes without saying, I think, that those who want to be redeemed are those who are bitten or cursed against their will.'

'And you think Phelan will have bitten someone else?' Evie felt nauseous. She nodded sadly. 'Yes, I'm sure you are right. The afflicted become wolves on the full moon, is that not right?'

'That is correct.'

'But both times when I saw Dolph and the others in the forest clearing, it was a full moon but they had not changed.'

'It is possible to control the metamorphosis. Some of those who wish to be redeemed have travelled many years in the Far East, finding ancient ways of calming the fevered soul. They are able to control the impulses to a certain extent. For others, like Dolph, staying human for as long as possible during the full moon is a game. They drink, which as I'm sure you know, dulls the senses, until they are no longer in control and they must change. The last one to change wins.'

'Like a game of statues . . . ' said Evie, dreamily. 'Yes, that is what I thought at the time. That Dolph seemed as if he were playing a game of statues. Holding himself in.'

'Holding the beast in,' corrected Raphael.

'You speak as if the beast is a separate being.'

'It is a separate being. It is a demon that lives within the host.'

'So if we found Phelan whilst he was a werewolf, would he know us?'

'There is some evidence that werewolves retain a sense of recognition, yes. It's a basic thing, like the snapshot of a memory — but do not think that would save you, Evie.'

'You know what I'm going to ask next, don't you?'

'You want to know how you can save him. Haven't I already told you that you can't?'

'There must be a way.' Evie could hardly believe she was thinking about it, but it might be a way to set her brother free. 'If he dies . . .'

'His soul goes straight to Hell.'

'But that's going to happen anyway, isn't it? Sooner or later. Or do werewolves live forever?'

'They don't live forever, but they can live for a very long time, due to their body's ability to heal itself. It's possible that when you find your brother he will not look many years older than he did when you last saw him. The disease slows down the ageing process, but does not lead to immortality. A werewolf can be killed, but only through an injury to the heart or to the brain.'

Evie closed her eyes. There was so much to take in. Some of it she had read in reference books, but Raphael had clarified much that had seemed confusing to her, such as the many myths surrounding the wolf men.

'They say that a werewolf can be killed by a silver bullet. Is that true?' she asked now.

'Yes, but it has to be fired into the heart or into the head. Can you do that to your brother, Evie?'

She shook her head. 'No, but I thought . . .'

Raphael shook his head violently. 'I

am no assassin, and if you came here believing so, then you had best go and find someone else.'

'That's not what I've heard about you,' she said. 'They say that you hunt down these creatures and others that most people think of as belonging to myth and legend.'

'I hunt those who are causing too much trouble in certain areas, yes, but I do not set out to kill. I set out to negotiate. Sometimes, when in human form, they can be reasoned with. Not always, but sometimes.'

'I thought that if Phelan died, then at least my father might be at rest. He does not know what we know about werewolves. He will only see it as a blessed relief from Phelan's affliction.' Tears filled her eyes. 'Oh, I know what I'm saying is outrageous, and I hate myself for it. I know I would be damned too, but I've just spent the last few years watching my mother waste away, and my father is soon to follow her, I'm sure of it. I shall be alone and . . . ' Sobs that Evie had held in check for many months erupted from her.

He let her cry, and she was glad that he did not utter the sort of platitudes people normally do in that situation. No doubt he thought she was acting just like every other silly woman he knew.

'Please forget what I asked,' she said, when she had calmed herself. 'It was wicked of me. Wicked! But there must be some other way to save my brother.'

'There is, but it still involves killing another,' Raphael said grimly.

'How? You must tell me.'

'If you destroy the alpha wolf, then the beta will be cured.'

'The alpha? What does that mean?'

'It is the leader of the pack. The one with whom the disease starts. He bites others, who are the beta wolves. But it always starts with the alpha, so even if one is bitten by a beta wolf, destroying that beta won't save them. They have to find the alpha — the one with whom the disease started — and kill him. Then all the betas in that bloodline will be cured.'

'Dolph!' said Evie. 'Dolph is the alpha. So if he is destroyed, it sets Phelan free.'

Raphael did not answer immediately. He seemed lost in thought. When he did, he asked, 'How can you be sure that Dolph is the alpha?'

'Oh, he must be. He was the one that Phelan went to. He was clearly in charge of the pack, as you call it. Yes, I see now. We can save Phelan's soul, and bring him home.'

'You seem to forget that Phelan chose this path, Evie. He will not thank you for saving him. I should also remind you that whatever beast lives within Dolph, he began his life as a human being, and part of him still is human. A very flawed and disturbed human, but human all the same. Will your soul be any less at risk from destroying him instead of your brother?'

'He is evil. To get rid of such a man

would not be a sin. God would thank me for it.' Evie felt a sudden shiver down her spine, as if someone had walked over her grave. What she had said was blasphemy, she knew it, but the anger that had grown in her for the past eleven years was too strong for her to fight. She too had been haunted by her brother's disappearance, and even more so than her mother and father, because she had witnessed it and had been helpless to prevent it.

'Do you know how many wars have been waged with that same excuse?' Raphael said, darkly. He stood up and walked around to her seat, leaning over her and putting his big hands on her shoulders. The heat emanating from him seemed to burn through her layers of clothing. 'Knights going to the Crusades, burning cities to the ground and killing men, women and children, all in the name of God. Then there are other wars raged against countries accused of being evil, of not following the true God, when all the perpetrators really want is the land or the mineral resources. I do not say that some wars are not just, Evie, but do not invoke God in this crusade of yours. He may not be as forgiving as you hope.' Raphael's nostrils flared and she could feel his hot breath on her face. 'I told you many years ago that your temper would be your undoing. Rein it in now, or I will not help you to find your brother.'

'I'm sorry, but you cannot know how tortured I have been by what happened. By my own uselessness. I feel I have to put things right.'

'You are not your brother's keeper. You weren't then, and you are not now. I understand you wish to find him to set your father's mind at rest, but you must be aware, given what we have discussed, that this will not happen. Your father may end up just as haunted as you. Are you willing to risk that?'

'I think . . . ' Evie paused. 'I think I need Papa to see the truth.'

'Why?'

'For Mama's sake. She tried to tell him, but he would not listen.'

'If you care about your father, you'll let him die surrounded by his Gospels. The mythologies with which he is comfortable.'

'You call Christianity mythology?' Evie raised her eyebrow.

'It is not meant as a slight against your father's beliefs. As we both now know, werewolves exist, and they are considered legends by most people who consider themselves sensible. So why couldn't there have existed the kind-hearted son of a carpenter, who wished to bring peace to the world and save us from our sins? Ironic, isn't it, that so many wars have been waged in His name since? Even you invoke Him in your own crusade.'

Evie blushed. Raphael had a point. She had no right to involve God in her endeavours, or to use His name to justify her plans. Only desperation had brought her to this place — but that was still not a reasonable excuse for thinking of destroying another human being, even if that person was possessed by a demon.

'The next full moon is on the night of the twenty-fifth of December,' said Evie, thoughtfully. 'Christmas Day.'

'Yes? So?'

'If we can find Phelan by then, perhaps we can hope for a miracle instead.'

* * *

As Evie returned through the streets of Budapest to the hotel, she was ready to believe a miracle might be possible in what seemed to her to be a magical country. The snowbound city was decorated with holly wreaths, and the relatively new electric lighting gave the city a fairy-tale quality.

There were no Christmas trees. One of the staff at the hotel had explained to Evie that in Hungary, Christmas trees were not decorated till Holy Night. Parents put them up after children had gone to sleep, so that the little ones could believe fairies had left them. The man had also explained that here, Father Christmas, known as Mikulus, visited with gifts on the sixth of December, not on Christmas Eve. He was said to travel with a devil dressed in black who carried a switch.

'Mikulus gives presents to good children, whilst the devil beats bad children,' said the man. 'But as all children are both good and bad, they generally receive a present and a beating.'

Evie had winced, and wondered if that was what they meant by taking the rough with the smooth. The man had been so convincing that she had to remind herself this was just mythology; and that, thankfully, Hungarian children did not really wake up to a demonic beating. With a smile, she had to admit that the threat was probably a very good way to calm down excited children on the eve of Mikulus's visit. Her own parents' way of calming her temper and Phelan's bad behaviour had been to threaten to send for a policeman. Unless, she remembered with a frown, they really annoyed the reverend, in which case he invoked the fires of Hell.

Had Phelan been threatened with Hell so often that he had decided to make his own way there? No. She was adult enough to realise that her parents had made some mistakes in their upbringing, perhaps overwhelmed when faced with two particularly difficult children — Evie with her temper and Phelan with his sullenness — but her brother had been set on his path for so long, she doubted that anything they had said or done would have changed his mind.

Rather than go back to the hotel, Evie walked along the banks of the Danube, taking in the sights and sounds of the ancient city. There was no rush. Her father was sleeping, and she needed time to think. She found herself falling more and more in love with the city, and wished she had more time to explore it and get to know its warm-hearted people.

Attracted by the delicious smell emanating from a street vendor's stall, she bought a chimney cake: a Hungarian pastry shaped like a long tube and covered in sugar. She ate it as she walked the streets, her mouth watering with every bite. It felt more like Christmas than any December she had ever known. It hardly ever snowed at Christmas in England, even though it was the wish of everyone to wake up in the morning and find the landscape covered in white. Here was a place where she truly believed miracles might happen. Or perhaps that was just wishful thinking.

'Ah, Miss Price,' said the hotel clerk when she arrived back at the hotel. 'You have received some messages.'

'A message? That is very strange. No one knows we're here.' Except for their maid Polly. Evie hoped there had not been some emergency at home. She did not want to have to return when she was so close to finding her brother.

'One is from a Princess Alexia.' Did Evie imagine it, or had the clerk become even more respectful to her than before? As Evie had never heard of Princess Alexia, she had no idea how impressed she was supposed to be. 'Thank you,' she said, taking both messages.

The message from the princess was an invitation to a ball that evening. The other message was from Raphael. *We've been invited to meet with Princess Alexia, who may be able to give us some information. I trust you have something suitable to wear. I'll collect you at seven. Raphael.*

Evie touched the collar of her coat, perhaps hoping to find an answer there. She had nothing suitable to wear for an audience with a princess, that much was certain. She had never attended a ball, and whilst she had once seen grand ladies during a trip to London, she doubted she could ever look as elegant.

What did it matter, anyway? The

princess would hardly care what she wore. Nevertheless, Evie ran up to her room and frantically rifled through her suitcase in search of something even faintly elegant. The only thing she had was an old blue dress of her mother's, years out of fashion, but which she had packed to wear for dinner in the hotel restaurant.

She tried it on, and looked in the mirror. Despite the fact that it was perfectly acceptable back at home in the vicarage, here, with the idea of meeting royalty — and an unwelcome wish to impress Raphael — it looked shabby and old-fashioned.

An hour before the ball, feeling that she would have to refuse to attend, there was a knock on the door. The porter entered with a large box. 'A delivery, Miss,' he said.

Evie opened it up to find a shimmering white gown in the latest fashion, and a card saying: *I guessed you wouldn't have anything suitable. Raphael.*

She looked in the mirror at the shabby dress she wore, and wondered if he had noticed her clothes and been judging her all the time she sat in his office.

Her first thought was to tell him exactly what he could do with the ball gown. But she had never worn anything as beautiful. The girl inside her melted at the idea of putting on such an exquisite garment . . .

She decided she *would* wear it — but still make her feelings known to him when they met again!

5

Raphael arrived to collect Evie just before seven. Despite the reverend's concerns, there was little he could do but allow her to accompany Raphael to the ball alone. He had not been included in the invitation.

'I doubt the princess would tolerate an intruder,' said the reverend with a wry smile.

'It may lead us to your son,' said the Professor, as if sensing the reverend's concerns.

'You scrub up well,' Raphael said later to Evie, as they rode to the ball in a horse-drawn open sleigh. Bells attached to the horses' bridles tinkled as they moved. Evie and Raphael were wrapped up in piles of fur to keep out the cold. As in the afternoon, the sleigh ride added to the fairy-tale quality of Budapest, causing Evie to believe in miracles. In her fine gown, she felt she might well be a princess herself, perhaps escaping a wicked witch, with a handsome prince at her side . . .

She pushed the fancy aside. She had to keep a clear head. It was easier said than done, with Raphael sitting so close to her in the sleigh. Even with the fur coverings, she could feel the heat from his body. She had to remind herself that he was as far from being anyone's Prince Charming as it was possible to be.

'Is that a compliment?' she asked, frowning.

'No, just an observation.'

'I wish I could say the same for you,' she said impishly. She was forced to concede, albeit privately, that he too scrubbed up well. He wore an elegant black suit, with a crisp white shirt. A red sash lay diagonally across the jacket, on which were pinned several medals. But there was still a wildness about him that no amount of scrubbing up well could contain. It made her feel exhilarated and terrified at the same time. 'What are the medals for?'

'I've done various favours for the Austro-Hungarian Empire. Royal houses have a lot of secrets, and they pay well to keep them.'

'I thought you said you did not do this for money.'

'A man has to eat, and they can afford me. You obviously can't.'

'Because of my shabby clothes?'

'Ah, you were offended when the dress arrived. I thought you might be. I see you still wore it.'

'I had very little choice. I did not want to disgrace myself in front of the princess. But I did not come to Hungary to attend parties. I came to find my brother.'

'I agree. The reason I was able to procure an invitation tonight is that Princess Alexia may be able to help us find him. She has . . . contacts.'

'I've never heard of Princess Alexia. I looked up the current Austro-Hungarian royal family, but she is not listed amongst them.'

'In this part of the world, you can trip over princes and princesses on every corner. Not all of them are mentioned in the royal gazette. Alexia is one of the secrets they prefer to keep.' There was something in the intimacy of the way he said the princess's name that irked Evie. Not that she cared at all. Nevertheless, she pulled the fur covers closer as a sudden chill ran down her spine.

The palace was some miles outside of Budapest, but Evie did not mind. She was enjoying the sleigh ride too much, and wished they could just keep on going, at least until they ran out of snow.

'You won't find this palace in any guide books either,' said Raphael as he pulled into the courtyard. Other guests arrived at the same time, made up of ambassadors and politicians from all parts of Europe. The men were elegantly dressed in black, whilst the women wore the highest fashion. They were also all dressed in white. 'Princess Alexia always has a theme for her parties,' Raphael explained. 'And, as she hates the sort of petty rivalries amongst women about their fine clothes, she always insists they all wear the same colour. This year the colour code is black for men, white for women. It was another reason I doubted you would have anything suitable to wear.' Raphael got out of the sleigh and walked around to Evie's side.

Slightly placated, Evie took his outstretched hand and let him help her down. Her fingers trembled in his, but she put it down to the cold.

When they reached the ballroom, lit with hundreds of candles, she felt that the monochrome colour scheme gave the whole event an epic quality. The effect was almost that of dark and light clouds. When they occasionally came together, either whilst dancing or when a man leaned down to whisper in a woman's ear, Evie half expected to hear a thunderclap or see a burst of lightning. A Christmas tree at the far end of the ballroom was also decorated in black and white baubles, unlike anything Evie had ever seen.

'Are the decorations a Hungarian custom?' she asked Raphael.

'No. But Princess Alexia was never one to adhere to custom. Do you dance?'

'Yes. Do you?'

'Only when I have to.' He held out his hand for hers.

'Don't let me force you into it.'

He ignored her and led her onto the dance floor, sweeping her into his arms as a waltz began to play. 'Why the theme of dark and light?' she asked him, just for something to talk about whilst they moved.

'The princess believes that we each have dark and light within us. Good and evil. She is much drawn to extremes. Last year, she had all the women wear red whilst the men wore white. That signified fire and ice. Or sin and purity.'

'Ah, so you and the princess believe women are responsible for Original Sin?'

'I said no such thing.'

'Do you believe in redemption, Raphael?'

'I believe that sometimes in order for God to forgive us, we have to forgive ourselves. Until we do, then we cannot make amends for our wrongdoing. It's about accepting that we have done wrong and are ready to change.'

'What drew you to this life? I don't mean here, in the palace. I mean the life of hunting down werewolves and vampires and whatever other creatures are lurking in Hungary.'

'It's a long story.'

'I'm not going anywhere.' She wanted him to keep talking business so that she could ignore the feel of his arm around her waist. She had begun to notice that, even in the cold, he had a temperature far above the norm. Or perhaps it was just how he made her feel.

'It's not one I wish to share with you.'

'You could have just told me to mind my own business, then.'

'Mind your own business.' He said it without any malice, but it was still a firm refusal to share anything personal with her. She wondered what it was that he kept hidden from others. Although abrupt and outspoken, there was also a depth to him. She felt that she was sailing on uncharted waters where Raphael was concerned.

They danced for a while longer, before another man stepped in. Evie was dismayed by how easily Raphael relinquished her, but she noticed that he did not dance with another woman. He stood at the side watching her.

'How long have you known Raphael?' It took a moment for Evie to realise that the man with whom she danced addressed her. She was too busy watching the far more interesting figure standing at the side of the dance floor.

'Not long. We only met today.'

'That's quick work, even for someone like Raphael.'

Evie did not much like the man's tone. 'We are involved in a business transaction,' she said, blushing when she realised just how that might be taken. She was right to be concerned.

'Well, young lady, when you have finished your business with him, perhaps you and I could come to some arrangement.'

She blushed scarlet and her temper flared. 'I did not mean *that*!'

Within seconds Raphael was at her side. 'Excuse me,' he said to the man.

'Come on, Raphael, you can't keep this exquisite creature all to yourself.'

'How is your wife?' Raphael asked the man. 'Does she still believe you only visit Budapest for business? And, more importantly, is she still a good aim with a rolling-pin?'

The man let Evie go immediately and stormed away. Once again, she was in Raphael's arms, and knew it was the only place she wanted to be.

'You should be careful what you say to men like that,' he said sternly. 'He is the sort of man who thinks that all women are there for his enjoyment.'

'It is not my fault he is a cad.'

'No, but you should still be careful . . . ' He sounded unaccountably angry with her. He stopped suddenly, as if something had just caught his eye. He looked up towards the gallery where the orchestra played. 'The princess is ready to see us now.'

She followed his sightline and saw a ghost-like figure disappear into the shadows. Despite the heat from Raphael, she felt suddenly cold, and inadvertently moved closer to him to benefit from his warmth.

He took Evie to a side door, and up a staircase into a room that had a galleried rail overlooking the ballroom. It was adjacent to the minstrels' gallery, but not a part of it. A woman stood up and turned to face them.

She was probably the most beautiful woman that Evie had ever seen, with thick black hair, dark arched eyebrows and eyes of emerald green. She was also the saddest woman Evie had ever seen. Something in her eyes was dead, as if the emeralds had lost their lustre a long time ago. Her skin was deathly pale. She wore a white gown with a black sash around the waist, which only added to her pallor. Her lips, however, were the deepest red. Her age, like Raphael's, was hard to determine. She looked about twenty-five, yet her eyes were much older. Evie wondered what those eyes had seen.

'Raphael . . . it's been too long.' The princess held out her elegantly gloved hand and smiled, but it did not reach her eyes. Evie could not help noticing that the princess's canine teeth were quite long; the only flaw in an otherwise beautiful woman.

The atmosphere was heavy with some unknown quality, and she became convinced that there was something very intimate about Raphael's relationship with the princess. They did not just greet each other as old friends or acquaintances. There was something unspoken that made Evie feel like an interloper. It also annoyed her, for reasons she did not want to admit to herself.

Raphael bowed and kissed the princess's hand. 'It is good to see you, Alexia. This is Miss Price.' Evie, who had never met royalty before, gave a rather clumsy curtsey, but the princess was obviously too well-mannered to allude to it. She merely smiled again, her lips not widening quite as much as when she smiled at Raphael.

'Please, Raphael, Miss Price, sit down.' She indicated a plush sofa placed up against the wall, and took the seat opposite, facing them. 'Raphael has told me something of your brother's history, Miss Price. Perhaps you would like to tell me more.'

Evie quickly and nervously filled the princess in on what had happened to Phelan. Raphael helped her when she became stuck over the details.

'The dark and the light,' said the

princess dreamily when they had finished. 'Yes, we are all drawn towards one or the other.'

'It seems,' said Evie, sadly, 'that my brother never knew the light. Or, at least, he never let it in. Where my father was concerned, a child was either very good or very bad. He did not allow for the shades of grey. It sometimes seems to me that my brother, until he chose absolute darkness, existed in that grey area, without a foot in either camp. I was very naughty.' Evie grimaced. 'But Phelan was neither bad nor good. For him, choosing the darkness was an escape far preferable to choosing the light in the way my father sees it. My father isn't a bad man,' she added hastily. 'He just doesn't understand human nature very well. My brother might have looked for answers elsewhere, but because we were brought up in such an insular family, he had very little understanding of the other choices open to him.' She held out her hands as if to describe the weight of the problem.

'I'm sorry if I'm not explaining myself clearly.'

'On the contrary,' said Alexia, kindly, 'you explain it very well. It can seem as if one is living in limbo until one makes that decision.'

'But surely where he is now is a worse sort of limbo. Raphael tells me my brother may live for a long time, but when he dies he's damned. How can he believe the choice was worth the horror that awaits him?'

'When one plans for the future,' said the princess, 'one seldom sees past the day after tomorrow. Perhaps if you are lucky you can imagine life as far as next week or next month. But an extended lifetime before one is called to atone for one's sins? That is forever to most people. Until . . . '

'Until what?' asked Evie.

'Until one realises that the darker life is the real punishment and you don't need to go to Hell to experience it. Instead you endure a Hell on earth, looking for redemption.' The princess looked above Evie and Raphael's head, as if she had drifted far away into another place. There was silence for a long time.

Evie coughed softly. 'Raphael said that you might be able to help us to find my brother.'

'I know that with the full moon falling on Christmas Day this year, there is something brewing. It only happens every few years, and when it does, it means something important. I can taste it in the air. Can you taste it, Raphael?'

'Yes.'

'Taste what?' said Evie, a little annoyed at being left out. And yet, had she not tasted it too? It was the sense of foreboding that brought her to Hungary, along with the feeling that something of great import was about to happen. It was that certainty which helped her to sweep away her father's concerns, and persuade him to travel far from their home. Evie had to be there for whatever happened, even if she did not fully understand it.

'It is hard to say, but they are gathering, all of them,' said the princess. 'Not just the wolves, but witches, vampires, and other otherworldly creatures. Raphael, you remember my cousin Vladimir?'

'Yes, of course.' Raphael's tone was clipped, suggesting that there was little love lost between himself and the princess's cousin.

'He has a castle in Transylvania,' the princess explained to Evie. 'There have been stirrings recently. Villagers are moving out of their homes, scared off by some strange events in the forests. Go to Vladimir and he may be able to help you.'

'The last time I saw Vladimir he tried to kill me,' said Raphael.

'Only because you tried to kill him.'

'He deserved it.'

Once again, Evie felt like an interloper. Restless and unaccountably angry about the intimacy between Raphael and the princess, she stood up and went to the balcony, watching the dancers below.

She idly wondered if this was how the gods felt when they were looking down at the clouds from above, and began to understand why the princess arranged the balls. Alexia was like some other-worldly puppeteer, pulling at their strings, living her life through their lives. Evie suspected it made the princess feel more human to observe people going about their small, insignificant lives. Why she should have set the princess apart from humanity, she did not fully understand. But once the idea took hold, Evie could not shake it off.

'People-watching is fascinating, isn't it?' said Alexia. Evie jumped, not realising that the princess had joined her.

'Will you join them, Your Royal Highness?' asked Evie, already guessing the answer.

'No. I never attend my own parties. I merely like to watch. All of life is laid out before me. One does not always have to hear the words to know who hates who, which country is secretly plotting against another, and who is in love but cannot admit it yet.'

'Surely it is better to be part of life than apart from it.'

'And have you been part of life in that little village you come from, Miss Price? Tied to that dusty vicarage with your parents, whilst they grieve for a son who still lives, yet ignore the needs of the child they have in front of them?'

Evie spun around, her cheeks flaming. 'How can you know this?'

'Raphael told me.'

'How can *you* know this?' Evie said to Raphael, flashing accusing eyes at him. She had been stripped bare, and did not like the feeling at all. Despite her flashes of anger, it never occurred to Evie that her emotions were obvious to everyone around her. They were writ large in her expressive eyes.

'You told me. Perhaps not in so many words, but it was all there.'

'I think it's time we left if we're to set off for Transylvania early in the morning,' Evie said abruptly. It seemed that they were holding a mirror up to her, and she did not like what she saw. She was a girl who had allowed herself to become attached to a man she barely knew, to the point that she was already jealous of his friendship with the exquisite Alexia. But worse than that was them knowing of the pain of her virtual abandonment by her parents, who had only wanted their son to return so that their lives could really begin.

'You are not going to Transylvania,' said Raphael. 'I'll go alone and report back to you.'

'I'm coming with you, and so is Papa. It is my brother we're talking about.'

'It takes more than a day to get to Vladimir's castle. Your father is old and tired. I'd say that the trip to Hungary has taken most of his strength. As such, he needs rest, and he needs you to be with him. Where I'm going is no place for a woman. I have enough to do protecting myself. I can't waste time protecting you and your father.'

'I can protect myself and Papa. We are coming with you!'

Evie noticed that whilst she and Raphael argued about Transylvania, the princess watched serenely, with a small smile on her lips. She was a puppeteer, watching little lives unfold. Meanwhile, Evie and Raphael glared at each other, leaving much unspoken. It seemed as if the air bristled with electricity as they argued. Evie had never encountered someone who met her arguments head-on before. Her mother and father simply refused to listen to her concerns, sending her to her room until she was too old to be punished, and lapsing into silence when she became a woman. She had to admit there was something exhilarating about having someone argue back.

The blood pulsed through her body, and a vein on her neck began to pulsate, pumping the blood to her cheeks . . .

'I'm ready to be alone again,' said Alexia, suddenly looking very strained.

'Perhaps you can finish this argument on your way back to Budapest.'

'Yes, of course,' said Evie, chastened. 'Forgive me, Your Royal Highness, if I have acted inappropriately.'

'You have acted entirely appropriately, Evangeline,' said the princess. 'It will do Raphael good to be with a woman who argues with him. He is rather too fond of his own opinions.'

'What is this?' said Raphael. 'A lynch party?'

'Oh, look, he is really impassioned now. Behave yourself when you take Evangeline home, Raphael. I know that look in your eyes.'

Evie had too much time to ponder what the princess meant by that last remark as she and Raphael took the sleigh back to Budapest. She was dying to ask him about it, but guessed that she would once again be told to mind her own business. Finally, unable to bear the silence any longer, she asked, 'How old is the princess?'

'How old do you think she is?'

'She looks no older than twenty-five, perhaps thirty, but . . . '

'But?'

'She seems like an old soul. I know there are some people like that, but with her it's different. Why doesn't she ever join her guests?'

'She told you why. She likes people-watching.'

'No, it's more than that. When we were with her, she was fine at first, but then it was almost as if our presence became unbearable. I know the arguing didn't help, but I don't think that was it. Is she a werewolf?'

'No.'

'Is she immortal?'

'In a manner of speaking.'

'What does that mean? What is she?'

'What do you think she is?'

'Why do you keep answering my questions with a question?'

'Why do you think I do that?' His lips curved at the corner.

'I swear, Raphael, that if you tease me once more I shall push you out of the sleigh and find my way back to Budapest alone.'

They rode in silence for a while. 'Can I ask you a more personal question?' said Evie. 'No doubt you'll tell me to mind my own business.'

'The answer is: yes, we were romantically involved; but that was a long time ago, and we're not lovers anymore.'

'She's clearly still very fond of you. And you of her.'

'I'm one of the few friends who know her secret. That is the only thing that binds us now. She would be even more alone otherwise.'

'I'm sorry for her,' said Evie. 'I like her.' And it was true. Despite the strange emotion that gnawed at Evie because of Raphael's attachment to the princess, she had admired Alexia and pitied her loneliness. 'You say she is not exactly immortal. So does that mean that, like a werewolf, she can die, but ages slowly?'

'No. The princess is not immortal in

the way we understand it because to be immortal one has to be alive, with a pulse and a heart beat. Alexia has neither. She is undead.'

Raphael's words still made Evie shiver when she was in the warmth of her hotel room, several hours later. Vampires were said to be undead, cursed to walk the earth only at night, and afflicted with an insatiable hunger.

She began to understand why Alexia kept away from people. It must have been agony for her whilst Evie and Raphael were arguing in her sitting room and accounted for the sudden dismissal when, quite literally, their blood began to boil. Alexia had spoken about being in Hell on earth, and it seemed that was exactly what the princess had found by joining the ranks of the undead.

But for how long could someone deny the hunger of the beast within them? Ten years? Twenty years? A hundred years? It made her think of her brother. Even if she found Phelan and persuaded him to return home, how long would it be before the demon dominated him again? They might not only be putting themselves at risk, but also those who lived nearby.

Whilst her father had always dismissed their maid's stories of mutilated cattle and missing women, and Evie had tried for many years to rationalise it, she was beginning to wonder if all those things were really true. Despite her conversation with Raphael about so-called real werewolves, a part of her wanted to believe it was a mental affliction. Something that could be cured by modern medicine, rather than a very real curse from which there was no escape except death. And even death only led to damnation. What hope had anyone of redemption if they made the mistake of joining the ranks of demons?

She paced her room late into the night, on the one hand trying to convince herself that the old tales were merely fairy stories, designed to make sure the common people behaved themselves. But on the other hand, she still had the memory of seeing Dolph in the forest, seeming to grow in stature by the light of the full moon. Time, she decided, had played tricks on her mind. She could not have seen what she saw. Her memories were only those of an impressionable child and teenager. Dolph might be dangerous, and probably not the best person for her brother to be around, but was he really a demon with the power to turn her brother into one too?

And there was the fact that, despite Raphael's insistence that he wanted to shine light in dark corners, he completely accepted the fact of Princess Alexia being a vampire. Perhaps her editor had been right, and Raphael was a charlatan, fooling Evie with smoke and mirrors. Perhaps he had even conned the princess into believing she was afflicted. Or maybe they were in it together, with Alexia willing to do his bidding and put on a show for Evie.

That might also be the reason he did

not want Evie and her father to accompany him to Transylvania. He could return with any old story about his adventures searching for her brother, and expect them to believe it, then pay up.

Yet something about him compelled Evie to trust him. She realised she might be afflicted by the same stupidity that allowed her friends to fall for the wrong men, but there was something so forthright and honest about Raphael, sometimes to the point of rudeness, that it was hard to believe he would play such a game.

Whatever he might be planning, Evie made a decision to be with him every step of the way. If he was a charlatan, she would expose him. And if he was not . . .

She opened her trunk and took out a wooden oblong box. Inside it was a revolver. It was a woman's gun, small, with an ivory handle, and intricate carvings on the casing. Evie had bought it from a gunsmith in a city near to where she lived, but where she was not known. The gunsmith had been amused by her other request, but strangely enough not surprised. One might think there were demons running around Britain all the time.

She lifted the gun and felt the weight, shifting it from one hand to another, before putting it down on the dressing table. With trembling fingers, she took a red velvet drawstring pouch from the box, and tipped six silver bullets into her hand.

6

Evie finished writing the letter to her father, hoping that he would not awake before she left. If he did, she might not be able to bear to leave him. Raphael had been right. It was not a trip her father could make. But that did not mean she could not go.

The reverend had slept almost continually since they arrived in Budapest, only waking to take some food.

'It seems I'm too old for travelling,' he had said with a sad smile over a brief dinner the night before. It was Evie's opinion that her father was not too old for travelling. He was merely too saddened by losing her mother, and by her brother's continued absence from the family. He had lost some of the dominant qualities which had made her fear him for so many years, allowing Evie to manage him in a way she never thought possible. He might be disturbed by her absence, but she suspected he would accept it. At least, she hoped so. She did not like to think of him coming after her.

Her father would only slow them down, and she knew that, in his presence, she would never be brave enough to do what might have to be done. Like her brother, she was stepping over to the dark. She only hoped that when the reckoning came, it would be seen that she acted for the best reasons. But what had Raphael said about that? People had justified terrible acts for what they believed were the right reasons. It did not matter if it gave her father the peace he so badly needed.

She went back to the communal bathroom in the hall, and scooped up the piles of hair from the floor, catching sight of herself in the mirror as she did so. She did not look like a grown man, her features and build were too fine for that; but with her auburn hair closely cropped, she might pass for a teenage boy. She had put on a pair of her father's tweed trousers, a white shirt, and a pair of red braces. She topped it off with a dark jacket, and over that a thick black overcoat. She wore her own boots, because her father's were too big, but she doubted anyone would be looking at her feet.

She had never thought of herself as a pretty girl, because her father had always chastised her mother and Polly when they said so, insisting it would lead to the deadly sin of vanity. And even though both Raphael and the strange man at the ball had said she was pretty, she had not taken much notice. Therefore, it did not occur to her as she looked in the mirror that her high cheekbones and wide blue eyes were too striking to pass for a boy's.

She planned to dispose of the hair en route to Raphael's office. She did not want her father or the chambermaid to have the shock of finding it. It would only disturb the reverend more. Polly had always insisted on burning hair, due to some old superstition. Evie did not have time for that.

She left the note on her father's bedside, checking that he slept soundly. She had another note to leave for the hotel manager, asking that he ensure her father was given everything he needed. She included some money for any extras that might arise. She trusted, having met the manager, that he was a good, honest man and would do as she asked, not simply pocket the cash.

With one last regretful glance at her sleeping father, Evie closed the door, picked up her small suitcase and took her first faltering step into the dark . . .

It was also a step to freedom. Was this not what she had wanted all along? She had longed to be free of her responsibilities and to go wherever she pleased. No doubt she would be punished for it; if not by her father, then in some other way. By the time she reached the hotel exit, she was beginning to wonder if she had done the right thing. She took a few more reluctant steps, then a few more, each time getting further away from the hotel. She could not go back now. It would mean having to explain her short hair to her father.

It became easier as she reached the halfway point between the hotel and Raphael's office. She began to speed up. She was no longer walking away from her old life. She was rushing towards a new one.

Raphael had told her he would be leaving at seven in the morning. She still had an hour to catch him. Nevertheless, she ran through the early-morning streets, a little self-conscious about her new attire. Once or twice she was sure one or two of the traders setting up their stalls stopped to watch her pass by. Why she should feel so afraid, she did not know. What could they do to her? As far as she was aware, even if they guessed her gender, there was no law in Hungary that forbade a woman to wear a man's clothes.

When she reached the building that housed Raphael's office, she found that it was all locked up. She was sure he lived there too, and must be getting ready to leave by now. She wondered if he had slept late. It had been the early hours of the morning by the time they returned from the ball, so it was possible. As if it might open by magic, she tried the door, even though she had already ascertained that it was locked. Of course, it was too early in the morning for the main entrance to be unlocked. The other businesses which rented office space would not be open until nine o'clock.

She went around to the back of the building, and as she suspected, found a courtyard where the stables and several carriages were kept, including the sleigh in which they had travelled to the ball the night before.

The door to the back entrance was locked too, and there was no sign of anyone inside.

Evie heard a sound behind her and

spun around. 'Raphael?' An old man was sweeping out one of the stables. 'Excuse me,' said Evie. 'Do you speak English? *Anglais?*'

The old man shrugged and shook his head. He said something in Hungarian, which she assumed was that he did not speak English.

'Professor Raphael. Raphael. I am looking for him.' Evie realised, with embarrassment, that she was doing that thing too many British people did when abroad. Speaking very loudly and very slowly in the hopes that the man would suddenly understand every word she said.

'Raphael,' said the man. Evie gave a sigh of relief. At least he understood that much. 'Raphael . . . ' The man stopped to think for a moment, then spoke again. Evie was sure at first that he said 'gun', then realised he meant, 'gone'. He made a sweeping gesture with his hand, which made it look as though Raphael had flown away.

'Gone? Gone where? Where?' She

was doing it again, shouting at the top of her voice. She shrugged, hoping that her basic sign language would get across to the man.

The old man grimaced and shrugged back. 'Gone.'

'No, he can't have. He wasn't due to leave until seven, and . . . Oh, that rotten, dirty sneak! How gone?' she asked. 'I mean, how did he leave?' She began a strange pantomime of different travel methods. 'Horse?' She made the sounds of clicking hooves with her tongue and pretended to hold a bridle. 'Carriage?' How did one manage to mime a carriage in a way that wasn't the same as a horse? She pointed to one instead.

The old man laughed and shook his head. Clearly enjoying the game, he put his arms close into his body, keeping the lower parts flat whilst rotating them. 'Choo choo,' he said in high-pitched tones. Much the same way as children did when playing with their train sets.

'A choo-choo? I mean, a train? Wonderful, thank you!' Evie took some pennies out of her pocket and gave them to him.

Budapest was waking up as she made her way to the railway station, with more people and vehicles appearing on the street. The people were mostly of the lower classes, who were forced to get up early to pander to the whims of the richer inhabitants of the city.

A carriage dashed by her in the street as she crossed the road to the railway station, almost knocking her off her feet. Some early-morning stragglers yelled after it, in what Evie assumed were very uncouth terms.

When she enquired at the ticket office, she was told that the train to Bucharest would be there in just over an hour. She had no idea where to get off, but hoped that she might meet someone along the way who could tell her. If Vladimir owned a castle in Transylvania, it was probable that he was known in the area.

It surprised her that there was more than one service to Bucharest in a day, given how far away it was, but as it suited her purposes, she did not complain. She simply bought her ticket and waited on the platform, still hoping that her father would not wake up early and come in search of her.

It was a very chilly morning, and even in several layers of thick men's clothing, Evie shivered. Some vendors on the station sold hot pies, so she bought one. Not because she was particularly hungry. She was too churned up for that. It was because holding the pie kept her hands warm for a while. After several minutes, and when it was still lukewarm, she ate it, hoping that taking food might warm her up inside. It did for a while, but not much could keep out the severe chill of the winter morning.

She caught the train without mishap and sat in a carriage, which she shared with what seemed to be a farmer's wife or peasant of some sort; a young, reasonably well-dressed, lady who was caring for a small child of about three; and an old man, who looked like an office clerk. He slept most of the way. In the way of travellers all over the world, they did not speak to each other to begin with. They simply eyed each other up, with no one wanting to be the first to start a conversation.

Finally, some way into the journey the young lady spoke to Evie in Hungarian, looking at her from under her lashes in a way that was a little bit disconcerting.

'I'm sorry, I don't speak the language,' Evie said, smiling.

'You are Engleesh? But that is wonderful,' said the girl. 'I am governess and must teach my young charge Engleesh. But I do not get enough practice. Please, you help me whilst we travel?'

'I will if I can. It will be nice to have someone to talk to. How far have you travelled?'

'We come over the sea from Africa.

Vitali . . . ' She pointed to the little boy. 'This is Vitali . . . his Papa is very important ambassador. But now I must return the child to Romania as there is trouble in region we just left. My name is Natalia. And you are?'

'Ev . . . Eddie. My name is Eddie.'

'It is good to meet you, Eddie. You travel far too?'

'Not yet. I'm on my way to Transylvania. I'm glad there's a train. I wouldn't have liked to make the trip in a carriage.'

'We are lucky to get train,' said Natalia. 'If we miss it there is not another till tomorrow at the same time, and in this weather a carriage is too cold and take many days. I have orders to get Vitali home by quickest route. As it is, we must sleep on the train.'

'What about the early-morning train?' asked Evie.

Natalia frowned and shook her head. 'No, no early-morning train.'

'Sorry? You're saying there is no other train?' Evie remembered the carriage rushing past her and it all began to make sense. So Raphael had not left by train. He had hidden from her! He had probably put the old man up to lying to her, thinking that she would not bother to get the train alone.

She was on her way now, and he could not stop her. If she had to do it alone, so be it. 'Do you know of a castle owned by someone called Vladimir? He is the cousin of Princess Alexia. You see, I'm not sure where to get out.'

Not only Natalia, but everyone else looked up when Evie mentioned the castle and the names. They all crossed themselves several times. The farmer's wife punctuated her genuflection by spitting on her wedding ring several times and muttering '*Dracula*'.'

'*Dracula*?' said Evie. 'But that's just a novel by Bram Stoker.' She had read it when it was first published, being both thrilled and chilled by the story. She had also had to hide it from her father, who would have been horrified by the subject matter.

'Oh, Eddie, not fiction.' said Natalia. 'You cannot go there. It is evil place. Evil. The father of Vlad the Impaler was imprisoned there, and Vlad still walks the battlements, waiting to avenge his father. People fear they will be impaled if they go near there at night.'

'I think that would be rather noticeable in modern times,' said Evie. 'No one impales their victims anymore.' Nevertheless, the already cold carriage seemed to become even chillier. There was silence, and Evie got the distinct impression that she had upset everyone. She had to admit that, given everything else she had learned over the past few days, it was ridiculous that she did not accept what they were saying. There was still some part of her that hoped it was all a load of superstition, and that perhaps Phelan did have a mental affliction. That would make life much easier in the long run, but Evie guessed that from here on in, life was going to get stranger.

Already she could feel normal life

slipping away from her. Looking out of the carriage window, she had the sense of stepping back in time, as civilisation disappeared behind them, and they got into open countryside where any villages they passed seemed to belong to medieval times.

They travelled on throughout the day, only stopping occasionally at stations where they were allowed to get out and walk for a few minutes and visit the facilities. The little boy, Vitali, became understandably fractious, cooped up in a tiny railway carriage with nowhere to go. Evie was reminded of her own temper tantrums when he started screaming at Natalia in Romanian. Natalia's response was different to that of her parents. The young governess made it clear to him that his temper must stop, but in such a way that within seconds the child sat back in his seat, chastened and seemingly sorry for his behaviour. A few seconds later, he slipped his hand into Natalia's. He clearly loved her very much and wanted to stay on her good side.

'Let me help you with him,' said Evie, the next time he became irritated. 'Vitali? Vitali, listen to me.' She began to sing nursery rhymes to him, and taught him how to play pat-a-cake. He watched enthralled for a while before he started to join in the rhymes in broken English.

'Most men are not good with children,' said Natalia. 'But then most men do not sing like women.' She smiled and winked.

Evie glanced around the carriage, relieved to see that the other passengers were asleep. 'Is that what gave me away?' she asked.

'That, and because most young men flirt with me because I am pretty,' said Natalia, without a hint of shame. 'You are clearly not interested. Of course, you could be a different sort of young man. You are pretty enough to be so.' Evie did not know what Natalia meant by that and dared not ask. 'Your singing voice says otherwise. Are you running away from a forced marriage, perhaps?'

'No. We don't have forced marriages in Britain. At least, as far as I know. I'm looking for my brother. I have a feeling that, after what I told you about the castle in Transylvania, if I tell you he left home to become a wolf man, you will believe me.'

Natalia nodded seriously. 'Yes. I believe you. People here do believe such things, even if the government and the rest of the world would like to pretend that we are all civilised now. The old superstitions are not just there as warnings for naughty children. The superstitions are there because they are real.' Natalia's eyes widened, and despite her more cultured speaking voice, she reminded Evie very much of their maid Polly.

'I was supposed to be travelling with a man called Professor Raphael, but he left without me.'

'Professor Raphael?' Natalia smiled and nodded. 'I know of him. He is very famous in these parts. I have seen him. He is very attractive, yes? He visited my employer on several occasions. He is a man that can be trusted to get things done so that governments can go on pretending the legends are just legends. Some say he is a charlatan, and I think sometimes he lets people believe it. That way no one takes what he does seriously, so that he may go where he wants. You need not have travelled this far. He will find your brother for you, I am sure. He is a fine gentleman, but very different. Rough around the edges, perhaps, and not at all like any other men.'

'No,' said Evie. 'He is not like other men. What do you know of him?'

'Only that he is called in to help when the demons are too much of a threat to the public. Some live among us, quite happily, you know. They do not bother anyone. Oh, they may steal cattle from time to time, and get a little wild at certain times of the year. We consider it a tax for them leaving us alone. It is only when they harm humans that the Professor steps in.'

'Do you know that there's supposed to be unrest in Transylvania?'

Natalia nodded. 'Yes, I have heard. Thank the good Lord, we are not stopping at Huneadora. That is where Vlad's castle is. We go on to Bucharest.' Natalia genuflected again. 'It is not safe for you to go there alone, Edd — ' She paused.

'It's Evie,' said Evie, quietly so that no one else could hear, even though everyone else was sound asleep.

'Evie. It is not safe for you to go to that region. You should have listened to Professor Raphael. They say that the witches' council convened not so long ago, and that many of the supernaturals are on their way there for the full moon on Christmas Day. It is feared they will use our Lord's Day for some evil means. Others say a prophecy will be fulfilled.'

'What prophecy?'

Natalia shrugged. 'I do not know, but it has something to do with witchcraft.'

The train travelled on, past the

border and through stations that were often only tiny platforms in the middle of nowhere, with no ticket office and no porters to help with luggage. As they moved into Transylvania, Evie felt again that she was travelling back in time, to a place where nothing she knew and trusted existed. She put it down to tiredness and nerves. She lived in the countryside herself, and apart from the two episodes with Phelan and the wolf men, life had continued in a very mundane way, dictated by the seasons and the crops. True, there were superstitions and traditions in some of the more remote villages in Britain, but urbanisation and the factories had for the most part replaced imaginary devils with real-life fears. Electric light illuminated the darker corners, eradicating the fearsome shadows of the past.

In the bleak, cold landscape of Transylvania, she could believe that the supernatural held sway. Shadowy corners, free from electricity, were allowed to continue in darkness. No wonder people believed the superstitions and held on to them so tightly. There was a sort of comfort in knowing there was good and evil, and that evil always existed in the darkness. When all was lit up by electricity in civilised society, it was sometimes hard to tell the angels from the monsters.

It was night-time when they finally stopped at one station, and the farmer's wife woke up and got out, touching Evie on the shoulder as she passed by.

'You vant Hunyadi Castle?' asked the farmer's wife, holding the door open.

'Erm . . . yes,' said Evie. 'I want Hunyadi Castle. I think.'

'This is stop. Come with me, I take you there.'

'Oh, is it? Thank you. I'll just get my bag.' Evie had been sure the farmer's wife slept all the way through her conversation with Natalia. But she had also been certain that the woman did not speak English.

Evie grabbed her bag. 'It was nice meeting you, Natalia,' she said to her new-found friend.

'And you,' said Natalia. 'If you ever need a friend, come to Bucharest.' She quickly told Evie where her employer lived and worked. 'Come to either of those places, and they will tell you where I am. I hope you find your brother. God go with you.'

'And you too.'

Evie got down from the train and realised that she was not just taking a metaphorical step into the darkness, but also a physical one. She pulled her coat around her, but still shivered as the train began to pull away. She watched as it moved out of sight, feeling that it was her only connection with safety, and fighting the temptation to run after it and beg the driver to stop. Natalia had only been her friend for a short time, yet she already missed the girl's cheerful chatter about her life as a governess.

'You come now,' said the farmer's wife, sounding peevish. 'Hurry. It is bad night to be out. The spirits are abroad.'

As the woman spoke, Evie gasped, convinced she had seen such a spirit leap from the train some way up the track. Had she imagined it? It was hard to tell. Though the landscape was covered in white, the snow-filled clouds above blocked any light from the moon and stars.

'Where will I be able to stay tonight?' asked Evie. 'Is there a hotel nearby?'

'You stay with me.'

'That's very kind, but . . . '

'You stay with me.' The woman's voice was firm. 'Come, there will be warm fire and hot stew.'

It sounded very tempting. Evie had little choice but to follow the woman, especially as she had no idea where they were going and the train had already disappeared into the distance.

They walked for what seemed like hours, after which time Evie's feet and hands were frozen. Finally, they reached a small hamlet in the middle of nowhere. Candlelight shone in a few windows, and she could hear noisy chatter from what appeared to be the local inn. Looming above the village was a castle.

'Is that Hunyadi Castle?' asked Evie.

'It is. Come, we have food.'

'Perhaps I should go straight up there,' said Evie. 'My friend is going there and I'm sure to meet up with him.'

'Only fool goes to Hunyadi Castle at night.' The woman took Evie's arm in a way that could only be described as forceful. 'We are here now. This my house.'

Sure that the woman was only being kind, albeit in a rather dominant way, Evie followed her. There appeared to be one room downstairs and one room upstairs. The woman busied herself lighting a fire, placing a pot of stew over it. Very soon, the mouth-watering aroma of onions and meat filled the small cottage. She also made coffee; which, whilst bitter, was at least hot, and helped to warm Evie up a little.

'Stew ready soon. Drink coffee and sit by fire.'

'Thank you, you're very kind,' said Evie, sitting down in a rickety rocking chair. Despite the apparent benevolence, she began to feel uneasy about the woman. Her kindness had a rough edge about it. Evie supposed it was just a difference in culture. She knew people from Northern England who were just as abrupt in their speech, yet their gruffness masked the warmest of hearts. But she doubted any of them would trust their home to a complete stranger.

'I go out,' said the woman.

'Out? But you've only just got home. Don't you want some coffee?'

'No. I must go now. Sit there and we eat when I return.'

Evie had no choice but to obey. She certainly needed the rest after the long, cold walk. She sipped the coffee and felt her eyes begin to droop. The room became warmer, or perhaps, she thought, that was just her. A long sleep would be wonderful. She had not had much rest since embarking on the journey to Hungary, because she had been too worried about finding her brother.

She did not know if she dreamed it, or whether it really happened, but suddenly the door to the cottage burst open, and in what seemed like seconds later, she felt herself unceremoniously lifted from the chair, but had no strength to fight back. Her arms flailed as she tried to beat the stranger's back with her fists. Or at least she thought she did, but it seemed that her fists had turned into giant sponges, bouncing easily off the granite spine of the man carrying her. She hoped that the woman would return and save her.

Only then did she realise, as blackness descended, that she had walked straight into a trap.

7

Evie was aware of feeling safe and warm, lying in a big comfortable bed. But, as her eyes started to flicker open, she knew that she was not safe. Her coffee had been drugged and she had been carried away from the old woman's cottage by some malevolent stranger. Not only that, but the old woman must have arranged it all, and only gone out to tell the man where to find her.

The woman must have been awake for at least some of the time on the train, and heard Evie admit to being a girl. That was, if she had not suspected all along. There had been some strange looks between the old woman and the man in the carriage. Was he the one who had carried Evie off? She doubted it. He had been getting on in years, and was rather small and frail-looking. With a growing horror, it occurred to Evie that perhaps Dolph had found her and intended to kill her, just as Raphael said he might. But if that were the case, surely she would be dead already. He would not let her wake up, let alone put her in a warm, comfortable bed.

What had Raphael said about destiny? Even though she had been puzzled by his words at the time, she too had felt as if her life were moving towards some natural conclusion. She did not want that conclusion to be that she was left to die in a strange place whilst her father had to mourn the loss of yet another family member. She should never have left him, she saw that now. It was selfish of her to let her father struggle alone in Budapest. And she could not really pretend her reasons had been entirely noble, to find Phelan. She had longed for adventure.

Well, she had tasted adventure, and look where it had got her. Deceived by an old woman and carried off by some strange man. 'Fool, Evie,' she murmured under her breath.

She moved her arms slightly to see if they were bound, thankful to find that they were not. That must mean that someone guarded the door. There might even be someone in the room with her, in which case she did not want to let them know that she had woken, so she kept her eyes half closed, trying to look around the room through lowered lashes. It was daytime again, that much she could work out. Watery sunshine shone through the cracks in the curtains. The room, though plainly furnished, was clean and warm. A roaring fire burned in the hearth, and the aroma of fresh, warm bread emanated up through the ceiling.

Convinced that no one was in the room, Evie got up, swaying slightly as the effects of the drugged coffee still lingered. Her suitcase stood on a chair, opened, and it was with some consternation and a furious blush that she realised she was wearing her father's nightshirt. Someone had undressed her. The thought was too awful to contemplate. It suggested the man wanted her for some other reason than to kill her . . . Well, if he did, he would soon learn he had a fight on his hands. Evie was not prepared to give in that easily.

She went over to the suitcase and checked the contents. Surprisingly, the gun case was still there. So whoever had captured her had not searched her suitcase for anything other than her nightclothes. This was rather strange if she were a prisoner. But it was also strange that a prisoner should be held in such comfort. Evie took the gun out of the case and felt better for having it.

She wondered if she was still in the old woman's cottage, but something about the size of the room she stood in suggested otherwise. It was not a huge place, but it was bigger than the old woman's one downstairs room had been, and the walls seemed to be in better repair.

The latch on the door began to lower, causing Evie to raise the gun and point it at the door. Whoever it was, she had no intention of remaining a prisoner.

'You might want to load that before you shoot me.'

'Raphael! What are you doing here? Why have you kidnapped me?'

He stood in the doorway, holding a tray full of food. He sighed, as if she were acting very stupidly. 'I'm bringing you breakfast, and I didn't kidnap you. I saved you after you allowed yourself to be kidnapped. Now, get back into bed and eat your breakfast.' He put the tray onto the bedside table.

'Did you undress me?' Evie wanted nothing more than to eat the breakfast. The bread was making her mouth water. She remembered that she never had managed to eat the stew that the old woman prepared.

'Yes, but I swear I had my eyes closed the whole time. Are you hungry? I'm starving. It's been a long night.'

Evie sat on the edge of the bed and broke the bread, handing half to Raphael. He moved the suitcase and sat on the chair.

'I told you to stay with your father,' he said.

'And I told you that it's my brother that we're looking for.'

'What on earth have you done to your hair? Don't misunderstand me, it suits you short, but it was rather beautiful hair when it was long.'

'You said that a woman would be vulnerable.'

'And I was right. You walked straight into the old woman's trap. By the way, you look nothing like a boy, no matter how hard you try.'

'I fooled Natalia for a while.' It was a lie, but it made Evie feel better to say it if only to disagree with Raphael.

'Was that the pretty governess I saw you talking to? She obviously wasn't looking at you in the same way I do.'

'How did you know about Natalia? I thought you came here by carriage. In fact, how did you even know I was on the train?'

Raphael chewed some of the bread and swallowed it before answering, almost as if he needed the time to think about how he would answer. 'I convinced myself that you would go back and wait with your father once you thought I'd left. I rode past you in the street. Old Gregor, the groom, did his job well, and was paid twice — by you and by me. I'd travelled an hour when . . . '

'What?'

It took him a while to answer again. Evie got the impression that he was choosing his words carefully. 'I began to feel you drawing closer to me. Don't ask me how or why, but I knew then that you were on the train. So I headed for the next station as quickly as I could, just in time to join the train when it arrived. I was able to get on without you noticing.'

'Why didn't you just tell me you were there?'

'I recognised the old woman, and I knew she'd recognise me. She's a known witch around these parts. Strictly small-time, but she knows what's been going on, and she knew that she had to stop you.'

'I don't understand; why did she have to stop me?'

'Stop interrupting while I'm telling my story,' Raphael snapped, as if it was a subject he did not wish to discuss. 'Then she persuaded you to get out at the wrong station. I doubt the other passengers would have noticed in the dark, anyway. One station looks pretty much like another in these parts, especially at night.'

'Why would she do that? Surely it would have been quicker to wait till we got to the right station, instead of that awful trek in the cold we had to endure.'

'She might have thought someone was waiting for you at the next station, and dared not risk it. Unfortunately, I didn't realise you'd got off the train until we were on our way. I just happened to glimpse you by the light from the carriages.'

'It was you I saw jumping out! I thought . . . '

'You thought what?'

'That it was a spirit of some sort. Then I thought it was my imagination. But why didn't you say anything then?'

'I had no idea, in the dark, whether the woman had a knife or a gun held to your throat. So I just followed at a distance. Then I waited until she went out, and arrived just in time to see you falling asleep by the fireplace.'

'I don't understand. Why didn't she just kill me?'

'I've told you. She's a very minor witch. She wouldn't dare until she'd spoken to the elders about you.'

'But why me, Raphael?'

'Eat your bread and drink some coffee. I promise you it's not drugged.'

'There's something you're not telling me.'

'There's something you're not ready

139

to hear yet. Besides, I've been on guard all night. I need to sleep. I'll take the bed, and you can keep watch.'

'Keep watch for who?'

'Whoever it is who's trying to stop us finding your brother. I trust you're not going to go off on some fool's errand to Hunyadi Castle whilst I sleep.'

'Only if you promise that I can go with you when you do visit Vladimir. And no tricks, Raphael. No leaving early, or pretending to leave early.'

'Like I said the other day, it looks as though I have to accept destiny. The fact you're here seems to prove it.'

'What do you mean by that?'

'Come on, get off the bed. Let me lie down.'

Evie stood up, and Raphael went to lie on the bed, shutting his eyes. Evie could have sworn he slept almost immediately.

'What do you mean by destiny, Raphael?' she asked softly.

He opened his eyes a little. 'It means I'm stuck with you and you're stuck with me. For better or for worse. Wake me if anything happens. Preferably before anything happens. Oh, and another thing, Snow White . . . '

'What?'

'Don't go answering the door to old hags offering rosy red apples. You know how that story ends. It might mean I have to kiss you again, and I'm sure neither of us wants that.'

'God forbid,' said Evie, trying to speak lightly, but feeling as if he had just plunged a knife into her heart. 'Not that anyone could ever mistake you for Prince Charming.'

'That's the gratitude I get for saving your life three times?'

'Oh . . . well, thank you for that, anyway.' Why did he always manage to wrongfoot her? Evie snatched up a few garments and left the room in search of somewhere private to dress.

She went downstairs and found a living area combined with a kitchen, much like at the old woman's cottage, but larger and with better furnishing.

Some deer antlers and other animal heads on the walls pointed to it being a gamekeeper's cottage of some sort. She looked out of the window and saw that it was surrounded by trees for as far as the eye could see. Raphael must have carried her, and her suitcase, a long way. Even if she wanted to go to the castle, she knew she would never find her way out of the forest alone. He had chosen their hiding place well.

Her clothes were hanging on a rope in front of the fire, and had dried out thoroughly. Dressed in the trousers again, but with the clean shirt she had packed, Evie set about finding food for lunch. The larder was reasonably well-stocked, with bread and cheese, winter vegetables, a few potatoes and several large chunks of raw meat wrapped in newspaper. There was more than she and Raphael could ever eat, so hopefully the cottage owner would not notice if some of it was missing. She wondered what might happen if the gamekeeper came back, but assumed

Raphael had thought of that already, hence him asking her to keep a lookout. Where they could go when the gamekeeper returned, she did not know, but she hoped Raphael had thought of that too.

He seemed to have a sixth sense about most things. Including the fact that she had followed him, despite his best efforts to leave her behind. She smiled to herself. That would teach him that he could not boss her around. And yet, here she was, alone with him in a cottage in the middle of a dense forest. She was almost, but not quite, his captive. It was a clever prison. He must know that she would never dare leave there alone. Not that she wanted to leave. She had intended to find him and she had found him. He would know how to track down Phelan. She was forced to admit that without him, she was lost.

Evie did not have to call Raphael when the stew was ready. She heard his footsteps overhead whilst she stirred it on the open range.

'That smells good,' he said, when he reached the kitchen. He sat down at the table, which Evie had already set.

'It's a bit basic, I'm afraid,' said Evie, scooping food onto the plates. 'I don't know what half the herbs in the larder are, and I was afraid of poisoning us.'

'They're all perfectly safe, but it's best to ask me before using any. I may need them for other purposes.'

'How do you know the herbs are safe? Does this cottage belong to a friend of yours?'

'It's mine.'

'Yours?' Evie rolled her eyes heavenward. 'And I've been on tenterhooks all morning in case the owner returned and threw us out. You might have said.'

'You didn't ask.'

'Oh, yes; I forget that with you, it's a strictly need-to-know basis, isn't it? So where exactly are we?' She sat down and took a bite of stew. It was good, even if she said so herself. She was still hungry, despite the bread she had eaten for breakfast.

'We're in Transylvania, some miles from the Hunyadi Castle. No one knows about this place and I only use it once or twice a year when I'm in the area.'

'It's lovely. The cottage and the surroundings, I mean. I imagine it's beautiful in the summer. I wonder you can bear to leave it.' Evie took a plate from the table and gave Raphael a large helping of stew. As she was hungry, her own plateful was not much smaller. 'I warmed the bread over the fire,' she said, pushing the loaf towards him. 'Tuck in.'

'This is good,' said Raphael, after swallowing a mouthful of stew. 'Did you use all the garlic?'

'Er, no, just a couple of cloves.' Why did he always make her feel as though she had done something wrong? Even when she was trying to do the right thing.

'Good. Just don't use any more of it, alright?'

'I won't. Sorry.'

'It's not your fault, Evie,' he said, gently. 'You weren't to know. It's my fault for not warning you. The stew is good.' His voice had become placatory, and he looked at her with something like admiration.

They ate in silence, and yet Evie felt it was a comfortable silence. Afterwards, they drank coffee sitting near the fireplace. Evie sat on the rocking chair, which was much sturdier than the one at the old woman's cottage. Raphael pulled a chair up from the table and sat on that, with his long, lean legs stretched out in front of him. She darned her stockings and he read a book. They might have been a married couple, relaxing after a meal together, Evie thought, then pushed the idea away. She doubted Raphael was good husband material.

'Are we going to the Hunyadi Castle today?' she asked.

'Going in daytime would be pointless.'

'The old woman said that no one would be stupid enough to go there at night.'

'She's right.'

'So, are we going there tonight?'

'No, Vladimir is not there. I already asked around when I reached the village last night. He has gone on his travels somewhere. Probably Whitby. His family have a strange attachment to the place. I hear the fish and chips are good.'

'Whitby? Papa and I might as well have stayed in England and taken a trip up the East coast,' Evie said, smiling. 'So . . . ' She hesitated. 'How are we going to work things out here? There's only one bed.' She blushed, which was something she seemed to do a lot in Raphael's company.

'I'll take the night shift whilst you sleep, you take the day shift whilst I sleep.'

'Yes, that works. Good idea. Who exactly are we expecting to turn up?'

'Your guess is as good as mine.

They're far better informed than I thought where you're concerned, though I imagine Dolph has something to do with that.'

'Dolph . . . I keep meaning to ask you. What do you know about him? How do you know him? How did he become a werewolf?'

'Can I answer one question at a time?'

'Yes, of course.' Evie blushed again. 'Sorry, it's just that I feel he is the key to all this somehow.'

'Hence your silver bullets.'

'I'm not going to kill him.'

'Yet you still brought them?'

'I thought . . . I mean . . . I . . . ' Evie faltered. She had not decided if or how she would use the silver bullets. Only that she felt better for having them in her possession. 'Please, tell me about Dolph so I don't have to think about it. You say he's the alpha.'

Raphael went quiet for a moment, and then said firmly, 'You said he was the alpha. I didn't. He's the son of

Jacob and Rebecca Lyell. I presume you already know that.'

'Yes. They died not long after Phelan went missing. I know that Dolph was a bother to them.'

'He certainly was. From a very young age, he was a wild one. But even he is not to blame for this, as much as you would like to hate him. The story goes that, many years ago, Jacob Lyell's great-grandfather had an affair with a young village girl. She hoped they would marry, but great-grandpa had other ideas. He became engaged to the daughter of another landowner. The landowner's daughter had a large dowry, which the village girl didn't. What he did not know was that his original lover was a witch. All her family were involved in the Dark Arts. When she found out how he had betrayed her, she flew into a furious rage and cursed him and all his male descendants, turning them into werewolves. She then married another landowner, and gave birth to seven daughters, before she found out that her husband was having an affair. Her temper once again got the better of her, and she cursed him and his mistress in front of the whole town. Some say that she drew the very hounds from Hell. My guess is that she probably just made a few dogs bark with all the fuss she made. Nevertheless, she was arrested and tried as a witch, but died in prison before she could be brought to trial.'

Evie had the flicker of a memory. Something her mother had once told her, before her father had entered the room and remonstrated with Harriet for filling their daughter's head with such rubbish. 'My great-great-grandmother died in prison, accused of being a witch.'

'Yes, I know. Her name was Evangeline.'

Evie nodded thoughtfully. 'My mother named me after her, much to Papa's dismay. But Mama always said that it was meant to be, because I looked so much like her. My great-great-grandmother, that is. So what you're saying is that

Dolph could not be the alpha, because his father would be? But Mr Lyell seemed to be such a nice man. A little quiet and sullen at times, but there was no bad in him. He was well-respected in the area.'

Again Raphael was silent for a time. 'It is a little more complicated than that, and I'm too tired to explain. I'll sleep until suppertime, and then you can go to bed.'

He went back upstairs, leaving her alone in the kitchen, as she pondered exactly what he was not telling her. She had no doubt there was something missing from the story. She tried hard to think of the snippets of things she had heard over the years, both from her mother and from Polly. It had been difficult to learn much, with the shadow of her father's disapproval ensuring that such superstitions were kept to a minimum at the vicarage.

Much of it was as Raphael had said. Her great-great-grandmother had fallen in love with a man who betrayed her by marrying someone else, and she had put a curse on the family. Only, few people believed it to be a real curse. The Lyell family, though rumoured to be wolf men, had done nothing to prove the curse, so as the years passed by the story died away. Only a few people, like Polly, still clung to the old mythologies. Then Dolph started causing trouble in the area. At first he earned censure for fighting in the local taverns, and there was something about a young serving girl who had to go away and was subsequently disowned by her parents. It was known he and the others went to the forest to drink, having outlived their welcome in all the local hostelries, and that was when the legends of the wolf men started again. It was around that time that Evie and Phelan joined the story.

There was something else about Dolph that did not fit, but for the moment, Evie could not remember what it was. It niggled at her subconscious but would not come to the surface. Something she knew about him a long time ago, but could not recall. What was it? The more she tried to grasp at the memory, the more it slipped away from her. No doubt it would come to her in the middle of the night, when she was trying to get some sleep.

She sat in front of the fire as the shadows darkened, half-listening out for intruders and half-lost in memories. One memory led to another, and often she recalled things that had little to do with Dolph or Raphael: her own childish bad tempers, Phelan's sullenness, her father's intransigence, and her mother slipping into depression. It was all linked somehow, but in ways Evie could not connect. Not at that moment.

She believed Raphael when he talked of destiny. Her destiny had led her to this place, to be with him. Part of her wished they could stay in the cottage forever, cocooned from the world, but the story was not over yet. They were moving to some inevitable end and she was powerless to stop it.

8

Several days passed when Evie slept at night and Raphael slept in the daytime, only coming together to share meals, and for a few hours by the fire in the early evening. When she looked back on it later, she realised they were the happiest days of her life. With Raphael, she had the freedom to speak in ways she had never been allowed to before. Despite his apparent misogyny when they first met, he treated her opinions as those of an equal. True, they argued sometimes, but it was generally good-natured, and she was never told to be quiet or to not have an opinion. That was something that happened too much in her childhood. No wonder her temper had been so bad. So much must have been locked up inside her, because no one was able to speak freely in the vicarage for fear of upsetting her father.

It was ironic that being trapped in a small cottage in the middle of Transylvania afforded her more freedom than the large, oppressive rooms of the vicarage ever had.

Raphael was good company, telling her a lot about his life hunting demons.

'So, is Frankenstein real?' she asked him as they sat by the fire one night.

'No, it's a piece of fiction. Written by Mary Shelley.'

'I'm aware of that. I meant, is it based on anything real?'

'It is impossible to bring the dead back to life, Evie. Especially when they're a mixture of spare parts from lots of dead people. Medicine may be able to re-attach limbs — and one day replace major bodily organs, and I do believe we'll move towards miracles at the rate science is advancing — but it certainly was not possible in Shelley's time. Ask me about Cinderella and Rapunzel instead.'

Evie rolled her eyes. 'Alright, tell me about Cinderella and Rapunzel.'

'Well, Rapunzel was a game girl,' he said, his lips twisting wryly. 'Really liked to let her hair down, that one. But Cinderella . . . Phew! Give her a couple of drinks, and next thing you know, she'd be going home without her shoes.'

Evie threw back her head and laughed. 'You are incorrigible! Here I am trying to get an insight into your work, and all you do is tease me with fairy-tales.'

'There's a fine line between fact and fiction. All the Cinderella story tells us is that a woman has no chances in this world unless she finds a prince to marry.'

'I thought you'd approve of that, Raphael. Keep them from becoming journalists and all that.'

'I suppose it depends on whether I end up having to protect them.'

'You don't have to protect me . . . '

'No?'

'Alright, I got it wrong with the old woman, but it was probably a lesson I needed to learn. Not to trust anyone.

Everyone is entitled to make mistakes sometimes. Well, unless you're a member of my family.'

'And mine,' he said.

'What do you mean?' Evie listened avidly. Was he finally going to open up to her?

Raphael threw the last of his coffee onto the fire. 'Nothing. I'm just feeling sorry for myself a lot lately.'

'Why, Raphael?'

'Do you think your father believes that Phelan can really be redeemed? From what you've told me, he wasn't the most forgiving of fathers.'

'I don't know what he believes anymore. He's changed since Mama died. He's old and tired, and I think he's begun to question his attitude. Perhaps he realises that his austere Bible teachings and lack of unconditional love might have been what pushed Phelan away. Why do you ask?'

'I just wondered. If Phelan can be redeemed, perhaps there's hope for all of us.'

'You ... you're a good man, Raphael, even if you don't believe you are. Or maybe you just don't want the world to believe you are, for reasons of your own.'

'I told you not to get any romantic notions about me, Evie.'

'Oh, don't worry, I shan't do that. You're also arrogant, supercilious and abrupt to the point of rudeness.'

'Thanks.'

'You asked me not to romanticise you, and now you don't like it when I don't?' Evie raised an eyebrow.

'Yes, you've got a point. And you're right. I am all those things.'

'But you're still a good man.'

'Who knows? If you keep telling me that, one day even I might believe it.'

The conversation by the fire was the closest she got to finding out about the man beneath the gruff exterior. Despite his arrogance, he appeared to be filled with self-loathing over something she could not name. There was clearly much he did not tell her. Whenever she tried to press for answers, such as who his family were and how he became a demon hunter, he changed the subject, or insisted that either he was tired, or she must be, and that it was time that one of them slept.

He was a puzzle, and one she hoped to solve one day. He was sometimes rough in his speech, and often forgot the niceties — which she supposed came from him being alone for so long — but there was definitely goodness in him. She would not have imagined that spending hours locked up with one person could be enjoyable, but it was. At no time during the days in the cottage was she bored.

As they spent time together, her feelings for him grew, even if she denied them to herself. Yet he never touched her, and despite his gruff demeanour behaved as a gentleman, always respecting her privacy when she washed and dressed, and never trying to kiss her again. She would not admit to herself how sorry she was about that.

Their lives together over those days almost became domestic, and it was easy to forget, in this secluded cottage, that there was a world outside. There were books to read, and she took full advantage of those that were written in English. Most were about myths and legends. Raphael had written notes in the margins, but in a cipher she did not understand. She was tempted to ask him, but suspected he would only clam up again. She very quickly learned that he would only discuss his life when not pressed to do so. When she asked, he became defensive. So she just let him talk, hoping that one day he would trust her enough to tell her the truth about himself.

She had a stark reminder of the world outside early one evening, whilst Raphael was catching up on some sleep.

At first, she thought it was an animal howling. Only when the howls became louder, and started to sound like a chorus, did she realise that, despite the otherworldly nature of the noise, it was in fact coming from human beings. Or, at least, from beings who hid behind the pretence of humanity. The cries shattered the peace of the evening, sending shivers down her spine.

She ran to the window and looked out, but it was too dark to see very much. As far as she could tell from the sound, they were some way away from the cottage. Then, by the light of the half-moon, she saw shadows moving amongst the trees about one hundred yards from the cottage. The shapes seemed to shift and wane, and several times she felt sure that she only saw trees moving in the wind. But trees could not move with the same dexterity as the shadows did.

'Raphael . . . ' Her voice was barely above a whisper. She coughed and cleared her throat. 'Raphael!'

He was already halfway down the stairs when she called. He was topless from the waist up, his chest covered in a fine covering of dark hair. Evie did not know what she found more unnerving, the howling people or a half-naked Raphael. As the howls became louder, she decided to concentrate on them.

'Don't worry,' he said. 'They won't come any nearer.'

'How can you be sure?'

'I've set up a perimeter that they shouldn't be able to pass.'

'What sort of perimeter?'

'Let's just say it's why I prefer that you don't use up all the herbs and garlic. Plus, I've put a few bear traps further inside the boundary. It should hold them off, unless there are witches amongst them. But they won't dare come near.'

'Why not?'

'Because witches are mortal and I've got a big gun.' On saying that, he opened the door on a long, slim cupboard and pulled out a rifle, which he loaded. Then he put some wooden stakes in his belt. 'Put the candle out, Evie,' he said, moving to the window. 'And dampen down the fire. It'll be easier to see out, and it should be harder for them to find us. Let's hope there's a bit of cloud cover soon.'

She did as he asked, blowing out the candle, and putting some ashes from the grate over the fire to dull it a little. It was a cold night, and about to get colder, but with the blood racing through her veins, Evie felt very hot indeed.

'Now, go and get some garlic out of the larder, and put it along the bottom of the door and on the windowsills,' said Raphael. 'You'll find mistletoe and rye in there, too. Put the mistletoe above the door, and sprinkle the rye on the floor near to the garlic.' He gave her further instructions regarding some of the other herbs and spices in the larder. She understood none of his reasons, but obeyed him anyway.

'How do they know we're here, Raphael?' she asked, as she spread the herbs and plants around. 'You said that no one knew about this place.'

'No one does. They must have tracked us somehow. Or maybe they

163

just came across the perimeter and are wondering what's hidden behind it.'

'What can we do?' The howling increased in volume. Evie peeked out through the window, but could see nothing. She could only hear the otherworldly cries cutting through the darkness. 'I think they're nearer!'

'No, they're just louder. More have joined them. We sit it out till morning. Most of them are night creatures, so will disperse before the sun rises. The others, we may be able to get past.'

'I'll get my gun,' said Evie.

'You're wasting your time. I've taken the silver bullets. I don't want you shooting yourself in the foot.' All the time Raphael spoke, he looked out through the window. Once again, Evie had a strong sense of things he was not saying, rather than the words that came from his lips.

'I won't shoot myself in the foot! I have fired a gun before. I live in the countryside, remember?'

'You're not having the silver bullets,

Evie, and that's final. You may think you can kill another creature, but I am going to make sure that you don't.' He sighed. 'There's another rifle in the box. Load it and take guard at the other window. If anyone approaches on your side, don't stop to wonder why they're there. Just assume they want something bad and shoot them in the leg.'

'What happened to 'they're all human beings'?'

'They are, mostly, human beings; but if they want to kill us, I think it's best if we get in there first, don't you? And I'm not asking you to kill them. I'm asking you to maim them slightly.'

Once her gun was loaded, Evie took her place at the window. 'I don't see the point of shooting ordinary bullets at them if they're werewolves.' She looked at him accusingly. 'You told me in Budapest that the rye and mistletoe wouldn't work.'

'I told you they were superstitions. Just because someone becomes a demon, whether it be a vampire or werewolf, or even an addled old witch like the one who conned you into leaving the train, it doesn't mean that they lose those superstitions. Vampires can be destroyed by garlic and crucifixes simply because they believe they can be. Werewolves have an aversion to mistletoe and rye for the very same reasons.' Raphael shifted position at the windowsill, so that he could look out whilst talking to her. He spoke in a low voice, as if he feared those outside the perimeter would hear him. 'The mistletoe and rye is a phobia to them, like the fear of heights is a phobia to ordinary people. The human mind is a powerful tool, Evie. I've heard stories of men from native tribes who have been cursed by a shaman, and leave their tribe to escape the curse, travelling from place to place. Years later, in a different land, on a different shore, they've seen the shaman who cursed them standing over the road. Whether they really saw the shaman, or someone very similar, is uncertain. What *is* certain is that the power of the curse on the mind was so strong that they believed it enough for it to make them drop down dead in the street. It becomes a self-fulfilling prophecy. In much the same way that children who are labelled 'bad' in their youth often grow up to *be* bad.'

His words switched on a light in Evie's mind. It was only a half-formed idea, and she had no way of knowing if it was at all useful; nevertheless, it began to take root. She said nothing to Raphael, but stored it away as something she might need at a later date.

He was right about the mind being a powerful tool. She had often read about people, seemingly intelligent and sensible, who saw the Virgin Mary or Christ in everyday inanimate objects. Her father, despite his own beliefs, often dismissed such sightings as nonsense. But who was to say what looked and felt real to a person and what did not? It was only a matter of perspective.

Just as the lives of the supernatural were only a matter of perspective. They might simply be people who did not fit inside society's norms, so lived outside them, gaining legendary status from a public all too willing to believe in all manner of strange things when telling tales to each other on cold winter nights by the fire.

It was a long night, standing vigil at the window. The howling continued, as if those on the other side were trying to frighten them from the cottage. Evie was only brave on the surface because Raphael was. She did not want to disgrace herself in front of him. So she bit back the cries of fear that threatened to rise in her throat every time the howling grew louder.

Internally, she admitted she had never been more terrified in her life. But neither had she felt so alive. Was this the excitement her brother sought? For the first time she began to understand Phelan. Even the fear could become addictive; a way of jerking someone out of their mundane life. It was why some men became mercenaries. Not just for the money but for the excitement being a soldier brought them.

But could someone live like that for years on end? Always with their eye on the door in case they had to leave suddenly. Always set apart from society, until eventually there was nowhere they could go. Surely there came a point when they wanted peace, and to be able to sleep free from fear.

She rested her head on the window pane, and tried to switch off the sound. As a watery sun began to rise, she shut her eyes momentarily . . .

When she opened them again, it was daylight, and she was lying on the bed. She got up in a panic, wondering where Raphael was. She found him still standing at the window. He'd put his shirt and jacket on, which was much better for Evie's equilibrium.

'I'm sorry,' she said. 'I didn't mean to fall asleep . . . '

'It was dawn before you did, and I

think they'd gone by then,' said Raphael. 'There's hot chocolate in the pot. Why don't you pour us both a cup, and warm some bread over the fire? Then we'll move out.'

'What if they're still waiting for us there?'

'They probably will be, but we're not going that way. When we've eaten, we'll put a few things together and I'll show you the way out.'

'There's a way out? Why didn't we use it last night?'

'Because I needed them to see we were here all night, to lull them into a false sense of security. I want them to think we're trapped. They'll wait until the sun sets again, then they may try and break through the perimeter. Sometimes non-supernaturals join them and are willing to clear away the barriers. But they won't do it in daytime, in case they get shot. That gives us hours to get away.'

'You won't ever be able to come back here, will you?'

Raphael shook his head. 'Probably not. It's a pity, because I've enjoyed these last few days.'

'So have I.'

They looked across the room at each other for what seemed like an eternity. Evie's eyes went to the mistletoe hanging over the door. She would have liked to kiss him again, and wished he would kiss her. Only he had said he did not want that to happen. She lowered her eyes and set about warming the bread, losing herself in domesticity. The idea of them spending forever in the cottage, living off warm bread and hot coffee, whilst the world outside them changed, was very seductive. She gave little thought to the logistics of where the bread and coffee would come from, losing herself in the fantasy.

It was probably just as well they were leaving the cottage. Being there had lulled her into a false sense of security too. Several times she had forgotten all about Phelan and her father, because she had been so content in Raphael's company. It was like being a married couple, without the intimacy. If she were honest, that had been there too, hidden deep, like a promise of things to come.

Sometimes the bed had still been warm from when he left it, and she had lain there in the night, breathing in his masculine scent, and wishing that his whole body were there with her and not just his spirit. Her hands had traced the dent he left in the pillow, sometimes finding strands of his thick dark hair mixed with her auburn locks.

'I'm sorry we're leaving here,' she said, as she poured the chocolate. Her voice felt constricted. 'I'm also sorry that I can never come back.' She walked around the table towards him, and paused with his drink in her hand.

'Is that what you want?' he asked, softly, glancing above her head.

Evie looked up and realised that she had stopped directly under the mistle-toe. 'What? No, I . . . ' She almost stumbled forward and put his coffee down hard on the windowsill, spilling some over the top as she did so. Before she could move away he had caught her in his arms.

'Pity,' he said, 'because it's what I want.' His lips found hers and he crushed her to him. She felt the edge of his teeth brush her mouth, and in response, she nibbled his lips. The kiss was hungry, passionate, and carried all the feelings she had been suppressing. Her fingers found his dark hair, twisting the silky curls. His hands responded by stroking her hair, then her shoulders, tantalisingly skimming her breasts, then sliding down to her waist and hips.

Just as she thought she could quite happily be lost in his arms forever, he thrust her away from him and emitted the same animal growl he had used at his office, moving away with a speed that almost sent her flying. 'The sooner we leave, the better,' he said, throwing open the gun cabinet door, so that his face was hidden from her. 'Come on, we'll take the bread with us and eat on the way. Take only whatever you can easily carry by hand. Wear all your clothes if necessary, but don't bring your suitcase. We're getting out of here.'

Evie could only obey him miserably. She put on all her clothes, making sure that the gun was in the pocket of her coat. She fully intended to get the silver bullets back from Raphael at some point. She would wait till he was asleep. Why she had not thought about that before, she did not know, but it was an idea that helped ease the pain of his rejection.

Ten minutes later, they were ready to leave.

They left by the front door, but instead of heading into the forest, Raphael led her around to the back of the house where there was a storm door leading into a cellar. Raphael opened it and beckoned her to follow him. He lit a lantern and held it over the entrance, showing a large, cavernous cellar beneath the house.

'We have about five minutes to run as

fast as we can,' he said as he helped her down the steps. He moved the lantern and illuminated a tunnel on the far wall.

'You said they won't come until night-time.'

'They won't. Come on, we've wasted a minute already. Go on, you go first! Run!'

Evie started to run, hoping but unsure whether Raphael was close behind her. Sometimes she could see the light from the lantern, but other times it seemed to get further away. Every time she slowed down, she heard him yell 'Run!' so she had no choice but to keep going.

She had managed to run several hundred yards when she heard it: an enormous explosion behind them. Raphael rushed up behind her and hurled her to the ground as a ball of fire and dust rushed over their heads, taking a lot of the oxygen from the tunnel.

'They blew up the cottage?' said

Evie, trembling beneath him.

'No, I did. Hopefully it's blocked the entrance to the tunnel too. All they'll find when they come back is ruins. That's if they don't have a lookout. We need to get going. It's hard to breathe as it is.' He helped her from the ground and they began walking, with Raphael leading the way.

The trip was claustrophobic and practically airless. Eventually, after what seemed like too long a time, the air became clearer. Not fresh, it was too dank and musty in the tunnel for that, but at least it was easier to breathe.

'Raphael,' she said, when she could speak without trembling, 'your lovely little cottage . . . '

'Strange, I always thought of it as a miserable little place until recently. I can't deny I'm going to miss it. Maybe I'll build a replacement one day.'

Evie almost said that she hoped she would get to see it, but felt that she might be an unwelcome guest after the way he'd reacted when he kissed her.

She wanted to ask him about that. To find out why, when he had kissed her so passionately, he could just push her away and behave as if she had poisoned him. The question died on her lips. She was too afraid that the answer would be that he did not desire her enough, if at all. Their intimacy in the cottage, and the lack of a beautiful woman like Princess Alexia to entertain him, had no doubt fooled him for a while that he was attracted to Evie. Any port in a storm, and all that.

She tried to tell herself that it was the same with her. He was the only man within miles, and he had been kind to her, albeit in his brusque way. When she got back to civilisation — and it really felt as if they had left it a hundred years before — she would see other handsome young men and realise that Raphael was not that attractive. *Who are you kidding, Evie?* she thought miserably. He was more attractive to her than any man she had ever met, and going back to civilisation would not change her longing for him. She realised that her drug was not fear, but him. She was addicted to him, and she did not know if she could recover from her longing.

The walk through the tunnel took many hours. It was even longer than it had taken the old woman to lead Evie from the train to her cottage. Raphael would only allow short stops to eat the bread and drink from a flask of water. 'We can't be sure that the tunnel was blocked off at the other end,' he explained. 'They could have seen the explosion, then followed us in. Are you alright, Evie?' His sudden tenderness brought tears to her eyes, so she was glad that he would not see them in the gloom of the tunnel.

'Yes, I'm fine. Don't worry about me, Raphael.'

'I'm not worried,' he said, starting to walk again. 'I just don't want to have to carry you. Again.'

'I just hope you can keep walking,' she said, 'because if I had to carry you,

I'd probably just leave you.'

'I'll remember that the next time you need me to save your life.'

'I am grateful,' she said, blushing in the dark. Why did he always make her feel that way? 'To you for saving my life, I mean. And if I can repay you, I will.'

'Oh, don't mind me, Evie. I'm not used to talking to women. I tend to treat them as I treat men.'

'Even Princess Alexia?'

'She was a long time ago, when I still had some manners.'

'You're not that old, are you? Thirty-five? Thirty-six?'

He did not answer.

'Did you love her a lot?' Evie regretted the question as soon as it was out. It was a woman's question which revealed too much of her own feelings for him.

'I loved her enough.'

'What does that mean? Enough?'

'I loved her enough to care about her and treat her well, but not so much that it broke my heart when it ended.'

'I think that's how Papa felt when Mama died. I think he only just loved her enough.'

'Sometimes,' said Raphael, 'it's all anyone can ask of another person.'

'I think I'd rather be alone than be with someone who only loved me enough,' Evie said. She thought of the asinine Herbert, Lady Bedlington's nephew. She doubted he had any love for her. He merely wanted to please his rich relatives, in the hope of receiving more crumbs from their table.

'You might change your mind when you're older and you become lonely.'

'No.' Evie shook her head vehemently. 'I won't settle for second-best.'

'So what do you want, Snow White? Prince Charming riding in on his charger, declaring undying love?'

'I want someone who loves me more than just enough. I want someone who would be heartbroken to lose me, and I would want to be heartbroken if I lost them.' She could just make out the back of his head in the gloom, and knew in that moment that her heart was already broken. She had not really lost Raphael. She had never had him. Yet she loved him with all the pain of knowing that he would never love her.

It was not how she expected it to be: a sudden, rushing agony, which took her breath away and made her sob tears of anguish. Instead it left a silent, but deep and aching, void that she knew she would never be able to fill for as long as she lived.

9

The tunnel went on forever. In places it was narrow and hard to get through, even for someone as slight as Evie. Other times it opened out into large caverns, with several tunnels leading off. She trusted that Raphael would know which one to take, especially after the lantern ran out of oil and they were forced to walk in oppressive blackness.

Evie began to understand how mineworkers must feel, going down into the gloom every day. What a dreadful way to earn a living, perhaps never seeing daylight, because it was always dark when they came up from their shift. Never one to be claustrophobic, Evie now felt that if she did not see the sky soon, she would scream. Only fear of embarrassing herself in front of Raphael stopped her. She would not be the shrieking, simpering woman of this adventure.

Finally, and with a huge sense of relief, they emerged from a cave into a forest clearing. Evie had no idea if it was the same part of the forest where Raphael's cottage had been, or even another forest completely. Glancing up at the sky, and taking a deep, cleansing breath, she blessed it, despite the fact that dusk had arrived and it was not that much lighter outside.

She was surprised when, five minutes later, they left the forest and arrived in the village where the old woman's cottage was situated.

'Did you carry me through the tunnel?' she asked Raphael as they walked through the centre of the village. The castle rose above it, dark and brooding in the dusk.

'It was the only way out of the village without being seen.'

'You carried me, the suitcase and the lantern?'

'Not the lantern. I know those tunnels like the back of my hand and I have good night vision. I only lit the lantern today for your sake.'

'Won't the old woman see me in the village?' asked Evie, as they walked towards the castle.

'She won't come near you while I'm here. If she sees us going towards the castle, she won't come near us at all.'

Nevertheless, Evie was nervous as they walked through the village, expecting that someone would jump out and grab her at any minute. She need not really have worried. As Alexia had told them, the village was almost deserted. Only two or three men were in the vicinity and they seemed to have their own concerns, except for one old man who stood in a doorway, chewing on a pipe. His rheumy eyes watched them all the way up to the castle. As Evie turned back to take one last look at the village, he went inside and slammed his door shut.

'I feel like we should be carrying a bell,' she whispered to Raphael.

'Yes, they have a way of making you

feel like that around here. Especially when you have business up at the castle.'

'Why do people fear it so much? I admit it's rather grim-looking, but it's only a castle.'

'It's not the castle. It's the owner,' said Raphael. 'Then again, one could argue that the castle is as much part of him as his arms and legs. Without the castle, he is nothing; without him, the castle is just another building.'

'But the witch was afraid of it whilst you said he was away.'

'If you live in a place long enough and infect it with your own poison, it doesn't matter how long you leave it. It's there, waiting for you to return, and keeping out trespassers.'

The castle was a mixture of styles, brought about by each new generation adding wings. It was part gothic, part baroque, and part modern, but it looked as though it had not been lived in for some time, which rather belied Raphael's idea of it having the personality of its master. A moat surrounded it, with a drawbridge pulled up on the other side.

Raphael stopped just short of the castle moat. 'Do you have a crucifix, Evie?'

'Yes, of course. My father is a reverend, after all.'

'Then I suggest that if you're not wearing it, you put it on now.'

'I am wearing it. You said to bring anything I could carry.'

'Good. Whatever you do, and no matter what anyone else says or does, don't take it off.' He put his hands in his pockets and took out some garlic cloves. 'Put these in your pockets and keep them there the whole time we're at the castle.'

'My clothes will stink, Raphael.'

'Tough. Just do as I say. And stay near me the whole time.'

'Are you wearing a crucifix?'

'I don't need it.'

'Why not?'

'No one will be interested in me.'

'Why not?'

'Honestly, Evie, you're like a ten-year-old with all these questions.'

'I just want to know why I have to take precautions and you don't.'

Raphael looked squarely at her in the dim evening light. 'Because I'm not a virgin, alright?'

As Evie flushed scarlet, Raphael called across the moat, asking for the drawbridge to be opened. A few minutes later it was lowered, though when it was low enough for Evie to see the gate, no one appeared to be working the pulley. She trembled, and not just because of the snow on the ground and the chill in the air. There was something fetid about that air, and about the castle. She did not want to go in, but knew that she must.

Raphael jumped onto the drawbridge almost before it had touched the bank. Evie reluctantly followed him. They crossed the bridge and walked under the portcullis into a large open courtyard. A heavy creaking sound turned out to be a door opening on one side of the courtyard, once again managed by unseen hands. She spun around, hoping to catch someone, but whoever it was must have sunk into the shadows.

As fear gripped her, Evie slipped her hand into Raphael's. He gave it a comforting squeeze. 'You're safe as long as you stick with me,' he said, and she immediately believed him. He led her to the open door. They passed through several corridors, until another pair of doors opened, by hands unseen, into a large chamber. In the centre was a dining table, covered in dust, despite being set for three.

Around the edges of the chamber were ancient chairs and chaise longues. Several bookcases lined the end wall. A large fire burned in an inglenook fireplace at the other end, but it barely took the chill off the place. Evie guessed that the chamber was the only room in the castle in use, and even then not very often.

'I expected you sooner, Raphael,' said a disembodied voice, causing Evie to jump. A panel in the wall in the far corner of the room opened and an old man stood there, watching them. Despite the distance, Evie was sure that his shadow stood right next to her and that his hand was just about to touch her shoulder. When she turned her head and saw nothing, she put it down to a trick of the light. Yet still his closeness seemed to pervade the air with a thick atmosphere that made it difficult to breathe.

The old man came forward — except that Evie must have been mistaken about that too, as the man who approached them had a young face, with finely arched highbrows and an aquiline nose. He was pale, almost to the point of his skin being translucent, but his lips were deep cherry red. His nostrils flared as he reached Evie, and he smiled a little, showing the same overlarge canines as his cousin, Alexia.

'This is not a boy,' he said, raising an eyebrow.

'She's out of bounds, Vladimir,' said Raphael. 'So keep your fangs to yourself.'

'My, my, Raphael, we are getting territorial in our old age. I was merely enjoying the young lady's scent. Women are not as innocent these days, yet this one . . . '

Evie shivered again, but could not take her gaze away from Vladimir. Everything about him seemed to invade her, and make her feel vulnerable, even though he had neither spoken directly to her nor touched her. He held her captive. The worst of it was that she did not mind. He did have rather lovely eyes . . .

'Stop that,' said Raphael, snapping his fingers in front of Evie's face. She felt as if she had just been woken up from a long sleep, and recoiled in horror. How could she have thought Vladimir's eyes were lovely? They resembled a snake's.

'I'm warning you, Vladimir.' Raphael took a threatening step forward. He was twice the size of their ethereal host, yet Evie would not have liked to bet on who was the most dangerous.

'Warning me? In my own home? Is this any way to treat a friend, Raphael? Oh, but we're not friends, are we? Not since you tried to kill me. Yet now you need a favour from me.'

'If you're going to be awkward, I can find out what I need to know from someone else.'

'Please, let us be friends.' Vladimir smiled, and it seemed to Evie that it was the sort of smile a predator might have just before he ate his target. 'We are, after all, in the same business, Raphael, even if you insist on seeing yourself as different. Come, I have arranged food for your visit, and I shall sit with you whilst you eat.'

Whilst Evie wondered how Vladimir knew they were coming, it seemed that Raphael would not back down.

'Can someone please open a window?'

asked Evie. She coughed theatrically. 'I'm choking on the manliness in the air here.'

The tension seemed to lessen a little. Raphael backed down, but not before giving their host a last long warning look.

Raphael sat on one side of the table, Evie on the other, with Vladimir at the head. She noticed that when the food was brought to the table, Vladimir did not eat. He merely drank from a glass of wine that seemed to be a much deeper red than that of his guests.

'It is not drugged,' said Vladimir, when he saw both Raphael and Evie hesitating over their food and drink. 'As you know, Raphael, I prefer my prey to be very much awake.' His lips parted into the hunter's smile again.

'Or hypnotised,' said Raphael.

He sniffed at his own plate, and handed it to Evie, indicating that she should pass him her own. He also sniffed at that. He did the same with the wine. Satisfied that neither was drugged, he nodded to her. She was relieved, as the walk through the tunnels had left her feeling very hungry. The food was good, too, and she wondered who had prepared it, given that the castle seemed to have no servants. Perhaps it was the same unseen hands that opened all the doors. She shivered, and drank a little wine to fortify herself. She did not want too much, because even if it were not drugged, it might make her feel sleepy, and for some reason she believed it was better to stay awake in this castle.

'Can you tell us what's going on, Vladimir?' asked Raphael, when they had finished eating.

'It is the full moon on Christmas Day. It has all the supernaturals in a frenzy.'

'I had worked that much out myself. But why?'

'They say that something momentous is going to happen. Someone is coming, they say.' Vladimir looked at Evie. 'Someone who will change everything.'

'Like the Second Coming?' said Evie.

'Oh, no, child. Nothing Biblical. If it were, I would be worried about my own survival, yet here I am.' He smiled, but it held no warmth. 'This is about a prophecy being fulfilled.'

There was silence for a while, yet Evie could have sworn from the looks passing between them that Raphael and Vladimir were carrying on a secret conversation. Raphael did not ask about the prophecy, and Vladimir did not elucidate.

'What prophecy?' asked Evie, when she could stand the silence no longer.

'They say that someone is coming who will destroy the supernaturals' way of life, taking away all their powers.'

'And this is a bad thing?'

'Of course it is a bad thing for those who chose their path,' said Vladimir. 'Do you know why people choose to become vampires, werewolves and witches, Miss Price?'

Evie could not remember telling him her name, and Raphael did not introduce her. 'My brother did it to escape his life at the vicarage.'

'The world is full of people like him, who hate the idea of being ordinary. Of waking in the morning, going out to work, coming home, sleeping; with nothing to break the monotony, until they go to sleep when they are old and do not wake up again.'

'But life isn't like that,' said Evie, passionately. 'It doesn't have to be like that. What about love? What about the joy of watching your children grow? And then their children's children? What about striving to create something, whether it's a new machine, or a new type of flower, or a work of art? It seems to me from the little I know that all the supernaturals are interested in is destruction, and idling away their time drinking beer and playing games in the woods. How is their nihilism better than living a life full of purpose, and the chance to die without a stain on one's conscience?'

'Was your brother's life at the vicarage full of purpose?' asked Vladimir.

'No, I don't suppose it was.'

'Was yours, before you set on this adventure with Raphael?'

Evie had no answer for that. At least, not one she would share with Vladimir and Raphael. It was true that life had been mundane, and that in the past few days she had never felt so alive, so vibrant. And what had brought that about? Was it her brush with the supernaturals? Or was it just Raphael? All she knew was that the flashes of temper which had lain below the surface of her skin for too long seemed to have abated, because she had another outlet for her passions.

No longer did she have the sense of frustration that she felt whenever she was cooped up in the vicarage. Even being stuck in the cottage with Raphael for a few days had been more exciting than twenty-seven years with her parents. With him, there were no taboos. No subjects that one should not broach for fear of her father's disapproval. For the most part, she had been able to speak freely to Raphael and without fear of reproach.

Even here, in Vladimir's castle, was more exciting than being at home. The air crackled with some unknown substance which made her senses quicken. Evil filled the air, that much was true, but also something else. Goodness emanated from Raphael. It seemed to her that Vladimir existed in the shade, whereas Raphael was surrounded by light. She shook her head. It was ridiculous, because Raphael also had his moments of darkness. But were they any worse than hers, when she allowed herself to be ruled by her temper? Yet, she thought, she hoped, she was a good person.

'We're getting off the subject,' said Raphael. 'In particular, Vladimir, we want to know what Dolph is up to. Do you know where he is?'

'Dolph is at the centre of things, Raphael, just as you are.' There was something in the way Vladimir said the words that suggested more than the basic meaning. 'There is a meeting planned in a forest north of here on the night of Christmas Day.' He mentioned the name of a place which was unknown to Evie. 'You will find him there. But you cannot take her. You know that, do you not?'

'Believe me, I've done my best to stop her, and so did the old witch down in the village. But she keeps turning up.'

'Excuse me,' said Evie. 'I am still sitting here. Could you try not to talk about me as if I'm not in the room? And could we have less of the cryptic comments, please? They really are most annoying. It's worse than trying to solve a book of riddles. Why did the old woman try to stop me? Why did you try to stop me?'

'Because you're a part of it, Evie, whether you want to be or not,' said Raphael. 'I told you that it started with your grandmother. Well, it now appears it ends with you. Only we don't know how. All I know is that this Christmas you should have been safely at home in the vicarage, yet here you are. You should have stayed in Budapest with your father, yet here you are. And the old woman should have brought her friends to kill you, yet here you are.' He gestured towards her with his hand to illustrate his point.

'So why didn't you just leave me with the old witch?' she asked.

'They're the ones who want to kill you, not me. I'm not going to stand by and let that happen. All I've tried to do is keep you out of harm's way.'

'How touching,' said Vladimir, sipping his wine. A droplet rolled from the corner of his mouth and down his chin, making Evie feel slightly queasy.

'In your office, you said you couldn't fight destiny,' said Evie. 'Yet that's exactly what you've been doing in trying to keep me away from my brother and Dolph.'

'I told you I wasn't superstitious,'

Raphael said. 'At least, I wasn't until I met you.'

'As fascinating as this is,' said Vladimir, 'it is time for you both to sleep. I have placed two chambers at your disposal.'

'We're not staying here!' said Raphael.

'You will be quite safe,' said Vladimir. 'I give you my word.'

'Excuse me if I don't believe your word is worth much.'

'You will be safer in here than out there, Raphael, and you know it. Where would you stay? No one in the village will put you up now you have visited me. They won't know if you've been turned. And the nearest hotel is miles away. Do you not think you have made this girl walk enough today?'

Raphael nodded. 'Very well, but if you make one move towards her, I swear I'll put a stake through your heart.'

'You really never used to be so territorial, Raphael. Remember those twins from Bucharest . . . '

'That's quite enough. There is a lady present.'

'What twins?' asked Evie as they made their way to their bedchambers.

'There are some things you don't need to know,' said Raphael.

'Did you love them enough?' Evie asked, with more bitterness than she intended.

'Not nearly as much as I would have liked to,' he said with a grin. Her furious expression seemed to stop him. 'There were no twins. Vladimir is teasing you. Now, go to bed, and don't open your door to anyone but me. Make sure you keep your crucifix on.'

Evie's room had a large four-poster bed with thick red brocades standing right in the centre of the room. Lying upon it was a white silk nightgown, finer than any nightdress she had ever worn. She hesitated before putting it on, feeling that it might be better to stay dressed. But her clothing, which consisted of two shirts, a sweater, a pair of trousers, a jacket and an overcoat, felt heavy upon her. She had not been able to bring her nightshirt, so wearing the one on the bed seemed an obvious choice.

Obeying Raphael, she kept her crucifix on, although she could not help feeling that it seemed out of place with the low-cut, almost sheer nightgown. She clambered up onto the bed, and sank into the plush mattress. She had certainly never slept in a bed that fine. She felt like a princess in a fairy-tale. Pulling the covers up around her, Evie immediately fell into a deep sleep.

She dreamed of Raphael, but he always seemed just a little out of reach. If she could only get to him, everything would be alright. The past would not matter anymore, only the future. But in her dream, he made it clear that his future did not include her. One moment he beckoned her forward, but the next he held up his hand to stop her, a look of distaste on his face. She choked back a sob at his rejection, but this immediately changed to joy when

202

he smiled and beckoned her forward again.

Sometime during the night she became aware of the crucifix lying on her chest like a huge stone. It was so heavy, constricting her breathing. Surely it would not hurt to take it off for a moment. How could such a tiny piece of jewellery weigh so much? Her hand strayed to her chest, but she stopped. No, Raphael had said she must keep it on, even if it did seem to be crushing her.

But she could not breathe whilst wearing it. Surely Raphael would understand that she needed to breathe. Oh, what did it matter what he thought? He did not want her, did he?

'Evie . . . '

'Raphael?'

She looked up through half-closed eyes and saw him standing above her. 'It's alright, darling, you can take it off now.'

She tugged at the chain, and despite how heavy it was, it broke easily. She took a deep breath. That was much better.

'Darling . . . '

She opened her eyes again. 'Raphael . . . '

'Come to me, my love.' He held out his arms. Evie rose from the bed and went to him, feeling as if she floated across the room. She hesitated. Was he about to reject her again? He did not. 'I've wanted you so much, Evie,' he said, as he took her into his arms.

'I want you too . . . '

Something felt wrong, but how could it be wrong when she was in Raphael's arms, and his lips were caressing her bare neck? 'I love you,' she whispered. This was what she had wanted, to be touched by Raphael. His touch was compulsive, and yet . . .

'Are you ready to be mine for now and always?'

'Yes,' she said, faltering slightly.

'We'll be together for eternity.'

'Yes.'

No! she screamed inwardly. Something was wrong, yet she was trapped in the spell, unable to move from his arms. *What is wrong?* It was Raphael and he was kissing her neck. *Isn't this what I wanted?* But she did not want this. She only felt compelled to allow it to happen. There was none of the passion and longing she felt, only the belief that he held her captive, and that she must let him do whatever he wanted. That was not love. That was possession, and she did not want to be possessed.

His lips drew nearer to her jugular vein.

'I can't,' she said. 'It's all wrong.'

Before she could say another word, Raphael exploded into a ball of dust and drifted to her feet. She fainted, landing in that same dust.

10

Evie opened her eyes, and found that she was lying on the bed. Raphael — the real Raphael — stood at the side of the bed, his eyes alight with fury. Evie sat up and looked down at the floor, expecting to see the pile of dust. Had Raphael cleaned it up? Had there even been time?

'Vladimir . . . ' she whispered. 'But I thought . . . ' She could not tell Raphael what she had thought. It would reveal too much.

How long, she wondered, had he been there, waiting for the moment to strike? Had he heard her say that she loved him? Had he even seen what she saw? He might have only seen Vladimir kissing her, and her allowing it whilst declaring her love. Had any of it really happened? She could not be sure if she had dreamed it. If it was a dream, why was Raphael at her bedside, looking so angry?

'I didn't want . . . ' she started to say, only for her voice to die in her throat under the weight of Raphael's angry glare. 'He was going to bite me.' The stark reality of what nearly happened to her made her knees go weak again. She would have become one of the undead.

'With you wearing that nightdress, I'm sorely tempted to bite you myself,' said Raphael, sounding businesslike. Still, a dark fire burned behind his eyes. 'For goodness sake, get dressed, so I can start to feel sane and we can get out of here. It isn't safe.'

'But you've killed him.'

'No.'

'He's dead, really dead. Not undead.'

'You know when he said I tried to kill him before?'

'Yes?'

'He meant I *really* tried to kill him. I took his coffin out into the sunlight and opened it. One thing you must learn about the *Dracul* is that they always return. So we *really* need to get out of here, Evie.'

'If vampires always come back, what's the point of hunting them?'

'I'm not talking about ordinary vampires. I'm talking about the *Dracul*. They're the alphas of the vampire world, and cannot be destroyed. They can only be stopped long enough to give us time to escape. We won't have time to do that if you don't hurry up and get dressed.'

'I'm not getting dressed in front of you.'

'And I'm not leaving you alone. Besides, after seeing you in that nightdress, I promise you there's very little else you could hide from me.'

Evie's blush seemed to start at her toes. 'At least turn your back so I can have some privacy.'

Raphael grinned and turned around whilst Evie hastily dressed. She wanted to explain to Raphael what had happened. She had been fooled into believing Vladimir was him. But if it

208

had been a dream, Raphael might think she had feelings for Vladimir. If only she could be certain about what had happened.

'Where to now?' she asked as they walked back across the drawbridge. It was the middle of the night, and the few people left in the village appeared to be asleep.

'We need to find somewhere to hide until Christmas Day.'

'So Vladimir will be alright?'

Raphael turned and glared at her. 'Why do you care?'

'I do not care. I just think he cannot help what he is. That's all.'

'His family made a pact with the devil. He chose his path, just as your brother did.'

'Did Alexia choose her path? She said something about finding out that Hell was on earth.'

'Yes, she did. She was very young at the time, and wanted excitement. But as soon as she realised what eternity meant, she began to regret it. You've seen how alone she is.'

'Well, Vladimir is alone too. What's the difference between him and Alexia? Apart from the fact that you loved her.'

'Alexia has not tried to infect anyone else since the time she realised she had made the wrong choice. Vladimir . . . ' He paused and gave her a harsh look. 'I don't have to tell you about Vladimir, do I? You were clearly enjoying his attentions.'

So it *had* happened!

'I was not! I was mesmerised, perhaps, but I didn't want him to kiss me. I just couldn't move away.'

'I love you,' Raphael whispered, aping Evie's voice as she had said it.

'Yes, but I thought . . . ' Oh, what was the point? She could not tell Raphael that she had really thought it was him, and that it was him whom she loved. Not when he was clearly determined to think the worst of her. 'Why are you being like this? What is it to you, anyway? You're clearly disgusted by my kisses, so what does it matter to you if I enjoy it when someone else kisses me?'

Raphael stopped walking and turned to her. She was reminded of the time he had carried her home from the forest many years before. The moon was behind him, casting his face in shadow, but she could feel the anger emanating from him. 'Because I need to trust that you're not going to be seduced by every enigmatic being we may meet up with before we find your brother.'

'I assure you, I am not that easy.' How could she explain to him that all the time Vladimir had kissed her, in Raphael's form, she had known it was not him? Only, she had been trapped under a spell and could not escape. It was as if she was in a dream from which she could not wake.

'On the contrary. You've let me kiss you twice without putting up a fight, and Vladimir practically . . . ' Raphael stopped again, taking in a deep breath. 'I don't have to tell you what Vladimir practically did.'

'I hate you,' said Evie. She stormed off into the night, with no idea of where she was going. Tears of shame stung her eyes. She had not put up much of a fight with Raphael, that was true, and she had walked straight into Vladimir's trap. She would have to learn to be more careful in future.

She had only gone so far when Raphael caught up with her, catching hold of her arm. 'You're going in the wrong direction.'

'I don't care. Go away and leave me alone.'

'What? You're giving up looking for your brother?'

'No, I'm just saying I don't need you anymore.'

'Really?' Raphael spun her around and pulled her into his arms. 'Really?' He lowered his head and she knew he intended to kiss her to make his point.

With what seemed like superhuman strength, Evie pulled away and kicked him in the shins.

'Ouch! You little brat! That's two

kicks in the shins I owe you.'

'You don't think your kisses were punishment enough?' she said, archly.

That seemed to faze him for a moment. It was a while before he spoke. 'At least you're learning now,' he said, quietly. 'When we get to where we're going, I'll teach you some better blocking techniques.'

'I'm not going where you're going.'

'Fine, so we'll go wherever you want to go. Where do you want to hide?'

'You obviously mistake my meaning. I've told you I don't want to go anywhere you go.'

'Tough. I'm not letting you out of my sight. Because, whether you like it or not, whatever happens from now on concerns me too.'

'What do you mean? What has any of this got to do with you?' She recalled what Vladimir had said about Raphael and Dolph being at the centre of things. What had he meant by that?

'Never mind. I've got a friend who lives a few miles from here. He might be able to hide us. If we're lucky, we should be there by morning.'

Evie wanted to argue with him. She wanted to be away from him so that her emotions were not so churned up, and she could think more clearly about what to do about Phelan. But she also knew that she was a stranger in what was turning out to be a very strange land. She had no idea how to reach the forest of which Vladimir spoke, or what to do when she got there.

'Alright, I'll come with you,' she said. 'But I swear that if you try to kiss me again, I'll do worse than kick you in the shins.'

'Like you said, you've been punished enough.' Raphael's voice was filled with bitterness.

Evie had walked a lot in the countryside, but nothing prepared her for the treks she had to go on in Transylvania. First from the train to the old woman's cottage, then from Raphael's cottage to the castle, and now from the castle to Raphael's friend's house;

which, as he said, was several miles from the castle. Her legs complained loudly over yet another gruelling journey, but she did not want Raphael to think she was a weak, helpless woman.

'How can we possibly hide here?' she said, when they reached it. The house, which looked like a small keep, complete with turrets, was out in the open countryside with no cover for miles around.

'Hiding in plain sight,' said Raphael.

A large black dog ran from the house, barking furiously at them. It stopped a few feet away and stood there growling. Evie was convinced he would attack at any moment.

'It's alright, she's a friend,' said Raphael. The dog circled them, growling in low tones, before coming up to them and sniffing both their hands.

'Good boy,' said Evie, patting him on the head. The dog sat down and allowed her to fuss him. 'You are a lovely boy, aren't you?'

'That's quite enough!' said Raphael.

Oddly, he had the same look in his eyes as when Evie woke up from the spell cast by Vladimir. 'Go and tell your master we're here.'

The dog barked once and ran off towards the house. Seconds later a man came out of the front door.

He looked and dressed like a Cossack, and was even taller than Raphael, with high cheekbones and dark, slanted eyes. Despite his size and ferocious looks, he turned out to be warm and good-humoured. 'Raphael, my friend.' He and Raphael hugged, and he kissed Raphael on both cheeks. 'It has been too long.'

'It's good to see you, Sergei,' said Raphael. 'I see that you're still not too old to learn new tricks, either,' he added mysteriously. 'This is Miss Evie Price. She's a friend.'

Evie half-expected to be greeted in the same way as Raphael was, but Sergei just pumped her hand up and down, until she was afraid he might break it.

'You are hungry?' Sergei asked, patting Raphael on the shoulder with such force, Evie thought that he would knock him over. 'Of course you are both hungry. Raphael is always hungry, and you look tired, Miss Price.'

'Please, call me Evie.'

'Evie?' Sergei raised an eyebrow. 'And this is short for?'

'Evangeline,' said Raphael, before Evie could answer.

'Ah, so it has begun,' said Sergei. 'Interesting. I had heard of the prophecy coming true. There is much movement amongst the supernaturals. They head north.'

'I know,' said Raphael. 'We need to head there too, in a day or two. But we need somewhere to hide until then, Sergei.'

Sergei thought about it for a moment. 'My sister Tasha will help you. Come to the house and I will send a message to her. She is a witch, but a good one,' he explained, as he led them up to the house. It was cluttered but homely inside. A Persian cat lay sleeping in a basket in front of the fire.

Sergei prepared them a breakfast of thick bacon, with eggs and doorstep-sized chunks of bread and butter. Evie was so hungry, she ate everything put in front of her, wiping up the last bit of egg yolk with the bread so that her plate looked as clean as when Sergei had placed it on the table.

'Demon hunting makes you hungry, yes?' said Sergei, laughing in his good-humoured way. His whole body shook, and Evie felt sure the house did too.

'No, running away from demons makes me hungry,' said Evie. It made Sergei laugh for about five minutes.

After breakfast, she and Raphael explained about Evie's brother.

'Yes, I know of him,' said Sergei. 'They call him Dolph's lapdog. Everywhere Dolph goes, the little wolf goes. He does not speak unless Dolph tells him to, and is the one to do all Dolph's bidding.'

'Is he . . . ' Evie hesitated. 'Is he happy?'

'Your brother? I cannot say he is, no.'

'So there's a possibility he might want to come home?'

'It is not so simple, Evie,' said Sergei. 'The life he has chosen . . . ' He shook his head. 'There is no way back.'

'There must be. Raphael said that Princess Alexia realised she had made the wrong choice, and decided to change.'

'Only she cannot change,' said Sergei. 'Not really. The demon is still there, inside her, waiting for its moment to escape again. Is that not so, Raphael?'

'Yes, that's true. Only death brings true freedom.'

'But even the supernaturals fear death,' Sergei said. 'Because of what awaits them on the other side. So they do not want to take that way out. If you succeed in persuading your brother to return home, you cannot be certain that he will want to stay there. The demon is too strong.'

'But if Dolph is killed, then the demon would leave Phelan. That's correct, isn't it?'

'Dolph? No . . . ' Sergei rubbed his chin and looked at Raphael. Evie was not certain, but she thought that Raphael imperceptibly shook his head. 'I see. It is like that, is it? Yes, that is difficult.'

'Is this another one of those cryptic conversations?' said Evie. 'Because if it is, I'll go back to my plan of last night and leave without you, Raphael.'

'Dolph . . . ' said Sergei, speaking carefully. ' . . . Dolph is not the alpha. You know that he was not born into the Lyell family.'

'What?' Evie slapped her head with her hand. 'That's what I'd forgotten. That Dolph's mother was Mr. Lyell's second wife. She was a young widow with a child. So Dolph wasn't born with the curse to begin with.'

'It is a sad story,' said Sergei. 'As a child, Dolph was intrigued by the legend, and bitterly upset that he was not a true Lyell. He longed to be a wolf man. So . . . '

'He got someone to bite him!' Evie clapped her hands together. 'Who? His stepfather? But Mr. Lyell is dead now. So why hasn't the demon left Dolph and anyone he has bitten?'

'Because,' said Sergei, 'Mr. Lyell did not die from a silver bullet.'

'He took his own life,' said Raphael.

'So there is no alpha,' said Evie, frowning.

'Of course there is an alpha,' said Sergei. 'The role is taken by the next in the bloodline.'

'So then Dolph becomes the alpha?' Evie was getting very confused.

'We're wasting time discussing it,' said Raphael. 'Sergei, you said your sister would help us.'

'Tasha!'

The cat got up from the basket and left the room. A few seconds later, a young woman entered the kitchen by the same door. She had the same slanted eyes as her brother, and it seemed to Evie that she looked like a cat in human form. 'There is so much that is not spoken,' said Tasha, yawning and stretching her long, slender arms to the sky. 'If only people would say what they feel and think, instead of withholding it.'

It occurred to Evie that there was something strange about this brother and sister. She looked around and realised she had not seen the dog since they arrived. Now the cat had also disappeared.

'I know what you mean,' said Evie.

'Ah, but you are just as guilty, child,' said Tasha. It was strange to be called *child* by a woman who did not look much older than herself.

'I'm not holding back information.'

'Are you not?' Tasha looked at Evie for a long while, until Evie was forced to look away. In that time, she felt as if Tasha had learned everything about her. 'I cannot blame you. Men are so foolish about such things.'

'What things?' asked Raphael.

'Affairs of the heart. You think we women read minds, but we do not. Then you wonder why we are so reticent.'

'We're not discussing affairs of the heart,' said Raphael. 'We're discussing where we can hide until Christmas Day.'

'It is all the same,' Tasha said, shrugging.

'Why didn't Sergei tell us you were here?' asked Evie, wanting to change the subject. 'When he said he had to send a message, I thought he meant it would take a while for you to arrive.'

'I like to observe people before I speak to them. Now — ' Tasha clapped her hands together. 'Somewhere to hide. I know just the place. Why did you not think of the crystal palace, Sergei?'

'It is too remote,' said Sergei. 'And too many miles from where they want to be.'

'I think that is the best thing at the moment,' said Tasha. 'Whoever seeks them will look for them around here.

They may even come to our home. They know Raphael is our friend. I will take them to the crystal palace.'

'Not more walking,' said Evie, grimacing.

'No,' said Tasha. 'I suggest we borrow my brother's horses.'

An hour later, they waved goodbye to Sergei, who went back into the house. The black dog came out and ran with them for several hundred yards, barking encouragement all the way, before he turned around and loped back to his home.

It was late afternoon when they reached their destination. The snow had become even deeper, and the landscape barer. Evie wondered how they could possibly hide in this place. They were practically on top of the building before she saw it, and Raphael had to pull her back to prevent her from riding straight into it.

Towering above them was what could only be described as an ice palace, hidden amongst the snowy landscape.

Crystal turrets stretched up to, and reflected, the sky overhead. Evie felt as if she truly had stepped into a fairy-tale.

'It serves two purposes,' said Tasha. 'It cannot be seen until you are near it, and as this land is so barren, no one comes here. Crops do not grow and there is nowhere for animals to graze. There are no minerals to mine, so the government also leaves it alone.'

'It's perfect, Tasha, thank you,' said Raphael.

'It's wonderful,' Evie said, 'but won't we be cold?'

'No,' said Tasha. 'You will soon see that it is very warm. Everything you need is inside, and you can light a fire without worrying about it melting. It has been here for thousands of years.'

'What happens to it in summer?' asked Evie. 'Doesn't it melt then?' She got down off her horse and walked round the castle, looking for the entrance. Raphael and Tasha followed her.

'Like I said, it is a barren land, and

even in summer this place is not warm. No one comes here. My family have used this castle for many years. Every few years or so,' Tasha said, becoming more serious, 'our kind is hunted by the government, who do not like our ability to hide behind our other forms, and decide that we must be evil. If not for Raphael, the last time we would have all been killed. Now, as thanks, we offer you our protection.'

'Other forms?' said Evie.

'They're shapeshifters,' said Raphael, clearing up one of Evie's suspicions. She had still not been quite convinced, despite everything else she had seen. 'Sergei and Tasha can turn themselves into any animal they want.'

So that explained the black dog and the Persian cat!

'Thank you,' said Evie. 'I hope I can repay you for your kindness one day.'

'Consider the debt already paid by Raphael.'

'I prefer to pay my own debts,' Evie said.

Tasha smiled lazily, looking more cat-like than ever. 'He is going to find you a difficult one, I can see that. Let me give you some advice, Evangeline.'

'What?'

'Sometimes you have to let the man be the man. It hurts their fragile ego if you do not.' She winked and went back to her horse, climbing onto it in one easy movement. 'I must return to my brother before the spell I placed upon our home fades. There is food stored in the larders here. Help yourselves. Evangeline, you are about my size, so you will find clothes to wear in one of the bedrooms. Good luck with your quest!' Tasha tapped her horse with her heels and disappeared into the distance.

11

The palace inside was just as magnificent as outside. Enormous chambers made up the downstairs rooms, and many had ice sculptures set in the alcoves. Evie wandered from room to room, marvelling at the sculptures and the fact that even much of the furniture was formed out of ice, but thankfully covered in every type of fur imaginable. She wondered if Sergei and Tasha's family had created the sculptures and the furniture themselves whilst in hiding. It seemed a good way to pass the time.

Oddly, it did not feel as cold inside as it did outside. The packed ice seemed to be a sort of insulation. Raphael still lit a fire in the main chamber, and pulled one of the large sofas up to it so they could warm themselves.

Evie found the kitchen chamber at

the back of the palace. Most of the food was frozen solid, which explained how it had been preserved, but all the meat and vegetables had been prepared. Separating them from the ice-packed shelf was a problem, but she managed that with a large hunting knife. She lit the stove and set to work making a meal, still wondering why, with the stove and fire burning, the palace did not dissolve into a heap of water around them.

'Will Sergei and Tasha be safe?' Evie asked Raphael when they sat down to eat. 'It occurred to me that they should have come with us and hidden here.'

'They can take care of themselves,' said Raphael. 'The forms you saw them take today are not the only animals they can become. They're just their favourite forms. They can become birds, fish, and cattle. It wouldn't surprise me if anyone visiting Sergei's house only found a couple of old pack horses grazing in the yard.'

'Horses?' said Evie. 'Those horses we

rode here today . . . '

'Don't worry, you haven't ridden all the way here on Sergei's grandmother. They were real horses.'

'I'm glad to hear it! I don't know if I'm ever going to believe people are what they really seem again.'

'Welcome to my world.'

'I keep expecting to wake up in my bed and find that this has all been a dream,' Evie said. 'Part of me wishes it were. I wish that the first time I followed Phelan into the forest, I only dreamed it, and everything that has happened since. I fully expect to wake up at any moment, aged six and hearing Mama calling me for breakfast.' An unexpected tear rolled down Evie's cheek. 'Do you ever feel like that?'

'All the time.'

'You've never told me about your family, Raphael. What did your father do?'

'He was a farmer.'

'And your mother?'

'She was a farmer's wife. She died

when I was born.'

'Oh, I'm sorry. Is your father still alive?'

'No.'

'You must miss him.'

'I miss the idea of him, just as I miss the idea of my mother. But it's fair to say that my father was as much a stranger to me as my mother. He never forgave me for her death, you see. I was a big baby, apparently. I weighed nearly ten pounds. My mother, they tell me, was tiny. He thinks I killed her.'

'But that's not your fault.'

'I wish you'd been around to tell my father that.'

'So do I.' Evie choked back a few spoonfuls of stew, imagining the unloved little boy who had been blamed for killing his mother. Her own life had not been perfect, but she had always known her mother loved her, even if her father did not seem to. Somehow, a mother's love meant more to a child, and Raphael had not had that. 'I never asked you why you were there on the night that Phelan went to the forest. On both nights, actually.'

'I was looking for Dolph.'

'To kill him?'

'No, just to speak to him. To ask him to see sense. It seemed to me that, as he was giving people the choice of whether to become wolf men, rather than just attacking anyone, there must be some good in him.'

Evie put down her spoon. 'You're a strange one. You kill — or at least, as you say it, disable — Vladimir without a second thought. But you really wanted to kill him permanently. Yet you want to reason with Dolph and you're friends with Alexia, Sergei and Tasha. According-ing to Tasha, you saved their lives.'

'It's as I said to you at the beginning, Evie, they're human beings. They may also be demons, but they still have human feelings and emotions. And, just as with humans, there are good and bad demons. I only care about stopping the bad ones from hurting the innocent. Whatever you might have felt about

Vladimir . . . and I'll grant you he's a handsome, charming devil . . . ' Evie started to protest, but Raphael held up his hand. ' . . . he hurts the innocent. In fact, he doesn't just hurt them, he actively seeks them out in order to corrupt them and bring them over to his side. That is what I fight against. If I can reason with someone, I will. Anything rather than take a life. Believe me, I'm damned already . . . ' His eyes became dark and tortured.

'What do you mean?'

'Isn't anyone who takes a life damned for eternity?' That was not the right answer. She could see it in his eyes, but he had closed himself off to her. Would she ever really know this man? She wished he would let her into his world, but even though she had spent some time actually living in it, she still felt like an outsider.

'But you say you do it for good reasons.'

'The road to Hell is paved with good intentions, Evie. That's why . . . that's why I don't want you to take that path. You're a good girl. Sure, you've got that temper, but you also have humanity, regardless of what you think you'll do to your brother when you meet him. My guess is that, face to face with Phelan, you'll see the humanity in his eyes, and you won't be able to pull that trigger.'

'I don't know what else to do, Raphael.'

'There is an answer, but we won't know what that is until Christmas Day.'

'Maybe the three wise men will turn up and tell us,' said Evie, smiling sadly. 'Even with all this snow, it's hard to believe it's nearly Christmas. I feel as if I've left the world I know and entered a different one. Nothing is certain anymore.' She took a sip of hot chocolate. 'You were right, you know. I should have stayed with my father. I should have remained ignorant of all this. How can I go back to my old life knowing what I know? I'll never be able to look at people in the same way again. I'll be wondering if the milkman is a vampire, or if the lady at the post office is a shapeshifter. And if they're not, then life is going to seem very mundane.' She put down her cup and then pinched herself hard on the back of the hand. 'No, I'm still asleep, it seems.'

'Are you?' said Raphael, looking into her eyes. 'I'm guessing you're more awake than you have ever been.'

'Yes.' Evie nodded. 'That's the most frightening thing about it. This life is seductive and that frightens me.' Or was it just being with him that frightened her? Not that she ever feared Raphael would hurt her in any physical way. But her heart was as fragile as the ice sculptures around them. One push and it would shatter into tiny pieces.

Soon their adventure would be over, and — provided they both lived to see it — her time with him would be over too. She would miss his vibrancy and his sense of humour. No one in her life had spoken so honestly to her. That was seductive, too, and dangerous. Because she knew she would believe anything he told her.

Rather than sleep upstairs in the colder bedrooms, Raphael brought two mattresses to the big chamber. 'We'll both sleep in here,' he said. 'We're not going to be getting undressed, so you'll be quite safe.'

'Are we going to take shifts?'

'There's no need. As Tasha said, we're well-camouflaged here, and I'm sure she'll have put a spell or two around the place to keep out trespassers. Why don't you go and search for some clean clothes for both of us? I'll make up the mattresses.'

Evie found the clothes in one of the chambers. There were thick woollen dresses, complete with woollen stockings, for her; and trousers and jumpers for Raphael. She took them downstairs and put them by the fire to warm. Then, because she had not seen the entire palace, she went on a tour.

Upstairs was more basic, which suggested that when Tasha and Sergei's family were there, they too stayed in the one chamber downstairs. But in one room she found some items which delighted her.

'What on earth . . . ' said Raphael, when she came downstairs carrying a box full of baubles.

'Christmas decorations!' she said. 'We don't have a tree, sadly, but we can pretty the place up a bit. Oh, don't look so curmudgeonly, Raphael. We'll no doubt be in the thick of things on Christmas Day, so what's wrong with enjoying ourselves until then? There are enough stores for us to make merry. It's probably a bit too late to make a Christmas pudding and a cake, but we can improvise with an ordinary fruit cake.'

After five minutes of going around the chamber, singing *Deck the Halls* whilst putting up decorations, Evie was delighted when Raphael started to join in with a rich baritone.

'Christmas was always a good time at home,' she said, as she hung up the tinsel. 'Papa was always happier because the church was full, and I think for him it was a validation of all he believed in. Because at Christmas everyone believes in God, don't they?'

'Do they?' said Raphael, smiling. He had stopped decorating and stood watching her.

'Yes, I think they do. No matter how one feels the rest of the year, it's impossible not to be enthralled by the magic of Christmas. Even now I'm a grown-up, I sometimes find myself listening out for Father Christmas's sleigh on Christmas Eve.' She stopped what she was doing, struck by a sudden idea. 'Oh . . . no, it's probably silly, but I wondered if we could carve a nativity scene out of ice. To add to all the other sculptures.'

'It's worth a try.' Raphael looked around exaggeratedly. 'There must be some ice around here somewhere. I'll go and find a chunk.'

* * *

'Is that a unicorn?' Evie asked Raphael. She blew on her hands to warm them up. Ice sculpting was absorbing, but also very cold. Despite the chilly nature of their endeavour, they had spent a happy couple of hours sculpting, in between drinking hot broth and eating warm buttered toast.

'No, it's clearly an elephant. That's its trunk.'

'I don't think they had elephants by the manger,' said Evie.

'They had two of everything, didn't they?'

'That was Noah's Ark.'

'Alright, Miss Reverend's Daughter, so my Bible studies are a bit rusty. Actually, they're non-existent. My father wasn't much of a churchgoer.'

'Didn't he believe in God?'

'He believed in God alright, but he said that God had stopped believing in him.'

'Why would he feel that way? Because of your mother?'

'I suppose that was it.'

'I can't imagine not going to church,' said Evie. 'I suppose that comes from being a reverend's daughter. We had very little choice. It was hard on Mama, though.'

'In what way?'

'She knew that Papa would always love God more than he loved her. More than he loved any of us. Phelan and I were a disappointment to him. I had that temper, and Phelan was always so sullen. Papa could never forgive us for behaving in the way children behaved. He's not a cruel man, so he would never beat us, but somehow his disapproval was worse. He wanted the perfect family, and instead got us.'

'There's no such thing as the perfect family. What is it Tolstoy says? That every family is miserable in its own way. At least, I think it was Chekov. My Russian literature is a bit rusty, along with my churchgoing.'

'Is that true? About every family being miserable, I mean.'

'I suppose it must be, if you had an unhappy childhood, and I did.'

'I don't know that I was unhappy. Phelan was. Sometimes I think my temper helped me to ease the frustration. Not that I'm excusing it. Was your father cruel to you, Raphael?'

'No. It was worse than that. When he'd finished hating me for my mother's death, he became completely indifferent to me. Then he went out and found himself the perfect ready-made family.'

'He remarried?'

'Yes, to a young widow with a small son. He loved that boy more than he ever loved me. Oh listen to me, feeling sorry for myself.' Raphael threw down the knife he had been using to carve the sculpture. 'I've had a good life. I like what I do. I don't need my father's approval. I don't need anyone. It's time we went to sleep.'

'You always do that.'

'Do what?'

'Decide that it's time to sleep when

the subject becomes too painful for you.'

'Perhaps it's because that's what my father did every time I tried to speak to him. "Go to bed, Raphael."'

Raphael got up from the table and went to his mattress, throwing himself down on it. Evie also got up, but went to put some more logs on the fire before lying on her own mattress, just a few feet away from his. She covered herself in the thick furs.

'Raphael?' she said, after a few minutes. She glanced over and could see him lying on his back, staring at the ceiling.

'What?'

'Did you want to kill Vladimir because he was the one who turned Alexia?'

'No, that happened long before I came on the scene, and she chose that life as a way of escaping her normal existence.' Raphael turned onto his side and faced her, his handsome features illuminated by the firelight. 'I had some friends, who had a teenage daughter. She looked a bit like you were at that age. She was a sweet girl, and planned to become a nun. Vladimir stole her away and turned her into a vampire. But there was enough of her left to feel the shame of what had happened, so rather than give the demon inside her free rein, she simply stepped out into the sunlight one morning, ending it. I hauled Vladimir's coffin outside in an attempt to do the same to him. I didn't know then that it was impossible to destroy him completely.'

'And that's why you wanted to kill him this time. Because of that poor girl? You were really angry when you staked him. Despite what you said about buying us time until he returned, there was murder in your eyes.'

'Get some sleep, Evie.'

'Raphael?'

'What now?'

'What you said about me feeling more alive than I've ever felt is right. I like being with you. Even when things aren't going well, I can't think of anywhere I'd rather be.'

'Don't.'

'Don't what?'

'Don't get used to this. I'm not a good person to be around. When this is over, you'd be better off going back to the vicarage and marrying a nice handsome farmer.'

'There aren't any nice handsome farmers where I live. They're all about eighty years of age.'

'Then marry a rich old farmer with a bad cough.'

Evie laughed. 'I can't go back now. I've told you that. I don't mean I expect to be able to stay with you. I know you won't want me around. I'd only hinder you. But there must be something I can do. I could study myths and legends as you do and become an expert. You could teach me . . . ' She was intelligent enough to realise she had just contradicted herself. One moment she had said she did not expect to be in Raphael's world, whereas in the next she had asked him to teach her his trade just so that she could continue to be with him.

Raphael sat up. She could see him by the light of the fire. His face was dark and brooding. 'Don't you understand, Evie? I don't want you in my world. I don't want there to be any chance that I'll meet you again.'

His words pierced through her. 'You can't make that choice for me, Raphael. It's up to me what I do. What is it about me that you despise so much? Whatever it is, it didn't stop you kissing me twice. Or is it different for men? Are you able to kiss a woman even when you hate her? Or were you just testing how weak-willed I was?' She turned over so that she was facing away from him. 'I don't need you to teach me anyway. I can work it out for myself. If you hate me so much, I promise that once all this is over, I'll never bother you again.'

'I wish it were that easy,' said Raphael.

'Oh, it will be. I'll make sure of it.'

Evie fought back the tears, determined he would not see her cry. She had been so happy during the evening, whilst they were decorating the room and working on the ice sculpture. She had thought for a moment that they could at least be friends. She had harboured a fantasy that he would teach her all that he knew. Now she realised that would never be the case. For whatever reason, he disliked her.

She wished it were as easy to dislike him. She had every reason to. He was arrogant and brusque, and his life had turned him into a bit of a savage. Yet he was also brave and noble, with kindness hidden beneath his gruff exterior. He had cared about the young girl who was going to be a nun; enough to want to kill Vladimir for corrupting her. He had saved Sergei and Tasha's family from the government. He had also saved Evie's life, several times. He might not always behave like a good man, but it seemed that he was drawn to protecting goodness where he found it.

After a night of fitful sleep, Evie came to a decision. Raphael was right. She should return home and marry a handsome farmer. Or some other boring man with no imagination. She knew that she could never have a foot in Raphael's world without always looking out for him, hoping that she would turn a corner and come face to face with him and find that he was pleased to see her. He had made it clear that he would not be. Better to grow old and die of boredom than to go through that agony.

With any luck, she thought, unwittingly pinching her hand again, in a few years she would wake up one morning and decide that everything she had seen and done had indeed been a dream.

12

The next couple of days, as Christmas Day approached and the moon started to grow bigger, became strained. Evie and Raphael only spoke to each other when they had to. She noticed that he had become very still, which reminded her of something or somebody, but she could not remember what or who. All she knew was that if she accidentally touched him, he snatched his hand away as if she had scalded him. He prowled the palace like a caged animal, double-checking all the doors to ensure they were secure. Or, it occurred to Evie, as if looking for a way out.

He had promised to teach her blocking techniques, but when she mentioned it, he said: 'Some other time.'

There were books in the palace, but all in foreign languages, so Evie could not read them. She had to content herself with looking at pictures in the few that had them. She worked on the sculpture of the nativity from time to time, but it was not as much fun without him, and he did not seem inclined to join in. In a fit of pique one evening, when the strain got too much, Evie knocked the trunk off the elephant. 'Sorry,' she said, when Raphael looked across. 'It was an accident.' She ignored his raised eyebrow.

'Evie,' he said one night, when they settled down to sleep.

'What?'

'I'm sorry for what I said. I have no right to tell you how to live your life.'

She did not know how to answer him, so she simply said, 'Go to sleep, Raphael,' wishing she could take it back the moment she said it.

A few moments later she felt the weight of his body lying behind hers. He put his arms around her waist and soothed her as her tears fell. She turned to face him, and traced the outline of his face with her fingers, raking her fingertips through the bristles of his beard. He said nothing, just watching her as she touched him, but she could feel his heart beating against her chest, becoming more rapid as her fingers traced a line to his neck. He closed his eyes as she reached up and pressed her lips against his. She waited for him to push her away, or draw her closer. He did neither. He merely let her kiss him, whilst his hand rested on her waist, feeling heavier with each passing moment. Evie did not know where to go from there. She did not know what words she could say to let him know that she was his if he wanted her. She almost said, 'I love you,' but was able to stop herself at the last moment. Let him think she desired him as a man if it fed his ego, but she could never let him know that she loved him. It would give him too much power over her.

His eyes had become blackened pools, so she could not read his response to her touch. 'Raphael, please . . . '

At that, his mouth covered hers, whilst his hands explored her body beneath the many layers she wore. Somehow, as she became lost in his kisses and caresses, he removed those layers, one by one.

★ ★ ★

'Tell me how to please you,' she whispered.

'You already do,' he said.

She could hardly breathe, wondering what pleasures awaited her next.

'Raphael . . . '

'Evie, I'm sorry, I've gone too far. I . . . ' She thought for a moment he might pull away. 'Tell me to stop and I will.'

'I don't want you to stop.'

He moved away from her.

'Go to sleep,' he whispered. 'Give me some peace.' It was not said in an angry way. It was more of a prayer for release.

251

His hand tightened on her waist, then he let her go and turned over, but he did not leave her mattress. He let her sleep huddled up to his back, yet she had a strange sense of being abandoned.

In the morning when she woke up, he was gone.

Evie ran through the palace looking for him, sure that he had only gone to the kitchen to make breakfast, but he was nowhere to be found. She eventually found the note he had left her on the table, written on the blank page of an open book. '*I'm sorry, but I can't be around you anymore. You make me forget myself and I'm afraid of the consequences. Despite what you might think, I never want to hurt you as I know I hurt you last night. You'll be safe in the palace until after Christmas Day. I did not lie when I told you that you cannot save your brother. Go home, Evie. Have a good life with some handsome farmer. Raphael*'

He had scrawled a map showing her

how to reach the nearest railway station, so she could return to Budapest.

'How could you leave me alone here after everything that happened?' she whispered as a tear rolled down her cheek. Was it because he knew she was safe inside the palace? He had mentioned that Tasha put some spell on the land which kept people away. After Christmas Day, it would not matter. Whatever danger there was would have passed. But still, he had left her alone the morning after they made love. His betrayal stung her.

She spent the day making plans to leave on the morning of Christmas Eve. She had found an old map in one of the books, and had worked out where to find the forest of which Vladimir had spoken. She would go there alone. She did not have to do as Raphael said. She was terrified of being without him, but that did not matter. Even if he did not want to see this through to the end, she would.

Dawn was breaking when she heard the sound of horses' hooves outside. He had come back! Evie jumped up out of bed and ran to the door to see several horses approaching. Sergei was at the head of them, and beside him, a pale young man. She could not see his face clearly as he kept coughing into a handkerchief.

'Sergei, what is it?' she asked, as they drew nearer.

'I am sorry, Evangeline,' said Sergei. 'But they took Tasha . . . '

Evie looked from him to the young man, who lowered the handkerchief.

'Phelan . . . ' She almost collapsed with relief, still not understanding the meaning of Sergei's words. 'Phelan! It's you. You're here. Oh, thank God. Sergei, there's no need to apologise. You've brought my brother back to me.'

Or, at least, what appeared to be a shadow of her brother. He had changed a lot in the years since she had last seen him.

'Come with me,' said Phelan, who

seemed reluctant to look her in the eye. Two of the men on the horses behind dismounted and began walking towards the palace.

'Of course, but don't you want food first? You must have come a long way.'

'Evangeline, come with me,' said Phelan in waspish tones. Only then did Evie realise that Phelan had not come for a reunion. Her own brother meant to do her harm.

She turned and ran back into the house, closely followed by the two men. She reached the big chamber and threw the first thing at them she could reach. The nativity scene shattered in front of them, but they merely laughed and chased her around the room. One tripped over a mattress, which gave her some more time, but when she reached the door, Phelan was standing in her path. 'You must come with me,' he said.

'Phelan, why?'

'I . . . don't argue, Evangeline. Just do it.' His voice became churlish, but was immediately followed by him coughing into the handkerchief, as if talking were too much effort for him.

Evie felt a hard thump to the back of her head, before all became darkness. Her last thought was: *Oh, no, not again.* Except this time, it was most certainly not Raphael who would save her. He had left her alone . . .

She awoke as she was being carried through a forest, which she guessed was some way from the ice palace, if only because there was not as much snow. With her body slumped over the front of a horse, she felt sick and her stomach hurt. The movement of the horse did not help, and neither did the awful animal smell of the man riding it. She was afraid to try and move in case she fell off the beast and was trampled underfoot. All she could do was hang on for dear life until they reached their destination. It was growing dark when they did.

Finally, when she was sure she could stand it no more, they reached a clearing in the centre of the forest, which was packed with a dozen or more tents. There seemed to be something of a party atmosphere, but she doubted the people there were celebrating Christmas.

Evie was unceremoniously pulled from the horse, almost crumbling to the ground because she had lost her balance. Determined not to appear weak, she stood up and held her chin high.

A group of men and women sat in a circle around one man. Dolph Lyell. Unlike her brother, he had not changed. He had retained that stillness, which was somehow fused with an arrogant swagger.

'You idiot,' said Dolph, getting up and walking over to Phelan. 'I told you not to bring her here. I told you to kill her and to make sure you did it before Christmas Day. It was part of the deal.'

'I wanted to be sure you'd keep your promise,' said Phelan.

'Phelan?' Evie's eyes opened wide in astonishment. 'You're going to kill me?'

She realised she had no right to be shocked, considering she had also considered taking her brother's life. But her intent had been to free him from his torture.

'You don't have the courage to kill her, do you, little wolf?' Dolph laughed.

'Don't call me that name,' said Phelan. 'You only say it to mock me! All these years, you've promised me that if I just do one more thing for you, I can become like you, and each time you find another excuse.'

'I don't understand,' said Evie. 'What do you mean, so you can become like him? You are a wolf man, aren't you?'

Phelan shook his head. 'Not yet.'

'But I saw him bite you, Phelan.'

'No, you saw him whisper in my ear that he would do it as soon as you had been chased off. He said he didn't like an audience. It's only one of the many excuses he's been using for years. Now, Dolph, are you going to keep your promise or not?'

'I said you had to kill her.' Dolph

stood with his arms folded.

'And I said that I won't until you've given me what you promised.' Phelan was beset by another fit of coughing. 'I need it now more than ever,' he said, his voice raspy.

'What's wrong with you, Phelan?' asked Evie. Inside, she was filled with a huge sense of relief. Phelan was not a wolf man, which meant he was not damned. She did not have to kill him — or Dolph, for that matter.

The main problem was that they intended to kill *her*. She had to find a way to get out of that. 'Tell me, Phelan, what's wrong?'

'Consumption,' said Phelan. 'From this stinking life we lead. But if I were like him, I might not be affected. My body should heal itself after the metamorphosis. For over ten years I've done his bidding, going to the places where he dare not. He owes me.'

'I owe you nothing, little wolf,' said Dolph, sneering. 'I could snap your neck in a moment and you'd be gone.

The same with your sister here.'

'So why don't you just kill us?' asked Evie. She sensed there was some hesitation in Dolph's demeanour. His arrogance hid a deeply-held fear. She could see it in his eyes. Was he afraid of her? It seemed impossible to comprehend, but that seemed the only explanation as to why he did not just end her life immediately.

'I will kill you both. Tomorrow night on the full moon,' said Dolph. 'Take them to one of the tents and keep watch on them,' he said to two of the men.

Evie refused to see his reluctance to kill her as anything other than hopeful. She and Phelan were taken to a tent, where, apart from being awoken by her brother's coughing from time to time, she managed to snatch some sleep. She thought about Raphael, wondering where he was. Did he know that Sergei had betrayed their whereabouts? Phelan told her that Sergei had been allowed to go free, and told where to find his sister. The big Cossack had asked Phelan to tell Evie he was sorry. She believed he would be. He cared deeply for his sister, and it must have been an awful choice for him to make to betray Evie and Raphael. At least Raphael was out of it.

She awoke at dawn on Christmas morning to see her brother looking at her. She sat up and tried to tidy her hair. She had no idea why it should matter how presentable she looked when she died, but part of her did not want Dolph to see that she had been trampled with fear. She would go out and face him with her head held high, and looking as presentable as she could.

'Why didn't you kill me, Phelan? If you want what he has to offer so much?'

'I've seen enough killing over the years.'

'Yet you still want to be like him?'

'I want to live, Evangeline. That's why I left home. I had to be alive. I was suffocating at the vicarage. You know what it was like. You railed against it enough with your tempers and tantrums. I could not do what I wanted with Papa watching over my shoulder, quoting the scriptures at me.'

Evie shook her head. 'No, Phelan. I've been thinking about it a lot over the past few weeks. Do you know how I escaped Papa?'

'How?'

'I left him a note and walked out of the door to come and find you.' Evie sat up. 'You've spent so long blaming Mama and Papa for the way you were, but you didn't have to be like that. As a boy, you had more chances than I ever did to escape. You could have gone to university. You could have joined the army or the navy. You could have become a doctor and saved peoples' lives. You could have been a great scientist, or a good farmer. The whole world was out there waiting for you. But I think all that seemed like too much hard work for you. Instead, you chose to take the easy way out. You chose to become a wolf man, thinking that would bring you the excitement you craved. Now you live this miserable existence with the bunch of similar parasites that surround Dolph, and it's killing you, and you're still looking for the easy way out.'

'Where did all that come from?' said Phelan, his eyes flashing. 'I see the years have done nothing for your temper.'

'Of course I'm angry, Phelan. I have been furious with you for so long because you just walked away instead of facing life like a man. You left us, Phelan. You left me to deal with Mama and Papa alone, except they didn't want me. They only wanted you back. I had to care for them both, and I daresay that when this is all over, if I survive this day, I'll be the one expected to care for Papa. Do you know how unfair that is? I have a good brain, I'm probably cleverer than you are, yet I never had the chance to use it. You had choices, Phelan. It's your fault that you're where you are now. Not Mama's, not Papa's.'

'No, it's not my fault,' said Phelan, bitterly. 'It's yours.'

'How can it be my fault? I tried to stop you. I came after you then, and I'm here now. I came to try and save you, Phelan.'

'You'd have done better to stay away. Why do you think Dolph has kept me on a string all these years, Evangeline? It's because of you.'

'I don't understand. I'm no threat to Dolph. Or at least, I wouldn't have been if he hadn't taken you away.'

'Hasn't Raphael told you about the curse?'

'Yes, I know about Great-Great-Grandmother's curse, and that I'm somehow involved in the end. But I can't see how I have any influence on what happens here. If Dolph lets us both leave alive, he'll find that out for himself.'

'I'm not leaving, Evangeline.'

'You haven't taken in a word of what

I've said, have you? None of it makes any difference.'

'I am not going home to die!'

'Oh well, then, die here in the forest if you must. Just tell him I'm no threat to him and that he can let me go.'

'It's not that simple. What exactly do you know about the curse?'

Evie quickly went through the facts as she knew them, about her great-great-grandmother being twice deceived in love, and putting a curse on one of the Lyell men, whom she assumed was Mr. Lyell's great-grandfather.

'It wasn't Mr. Lyell's great-grandfather, Evie. It was Mr. Lyell.'

'What? But that's impossible. Mr. Lyell only just died, and . . . Oh.' Evie remembered what Raphael had said, about werewolves living a long time. He had said that Phelan would not have much changed; yet she could see, now she had more time to look at her brother, that he had aged, whereas Dolph had not looked any different. Mr Lyell, the last time she saw him, had looked about fifty years old, when in fact he was probably much older. 'Surely people would have noticed.'

'Of course they noticed, but people have a way of justifying that which they don't understand. They merely say that the family are long-lived. Plus, Mr. Lyell didn't go out amongst people much after his first wife died in childbirth.'

'What?' Evie's blood ran cold.

'She died giving birth to their son. Must be fifty or sixty years ago now.'

'You were telling me about the rest,' said Evie, her voice barely above a whisper. *It could not be, could it?* 'About why Dolph thinks I'm a threat.' She did not want to discuss Mr. Lyell and the wife who died in childbirth. It would force her to face the unthinkable, and she could not do that. She would not do that.

'When Great-Great-Grandmother was in prison, she started having strange dreams. She said that one day someone born of her blood would bring an end to everything the supernaturals knew. That child, she said, would bear her name.'

'Evangeline . . . '

'Yes.'

'Oh, but that's preposterous, Phelan. I'm not a witch. I can't undo magical things. I wouldn't even know how to try.'

'Nevertheless, everyone here believes it is possible. Including Dolph.'

'So, what do I do? Point my finger at him and he drops down dead?' Evie remembered the story that Raphael had told her about the people cursed by the shaman. 'Shall I try it when he brings us out to kill us? I'm sure it will give us a moment's amusement before we're dead.'

She laughed bitterly until tears began to fall. That Dolph should have been afraid of her, of all people, was the most ludicrous thing she had ever heard.

She finally understood what Raphael had meant when he said that the supernaturals were just as superstitious as those without powers. Dolph planned to kill her based on the ramblings of an old woman who had probably gone insane in prison. Correction: her great-great-grandmother had probably been insane for a long time. Lots of people were thwarted in love and had their hearts broken, but they generally dried their tears and got on with things. They did not put dreadful curses on those who hurt them, and apply that curse to the offspring. The sins of the father should never be visited upon the child, regardless of what the Bible said. And yet a child had been cursed. She took a sharp breath as the pain of what she had been denying for the past few minutes took hold.

They were called out of the tent, and made to sit in the forest for most of the day. Occasionally someone brought them food, but no one spoke to them. Dolph prowled like a caged animal, as if waiting for something. Finally, as dusk began to fall, there was the sound of someone approaching through the trees. Perhaps, Evie thought with a sudden chill, someone whom Dolph had talked into killing her.

A man appeared in the clearing.

'Hello, Dolph,' said Raphael.

'Hello, dear stepbrother,' said Dolph. 'I wondered when you would come to meet our destiny.'

13

The atmosphere was as thick as the snow that settled on the ground. Raphael and Dolph stood face to face, eye to eye.

'I notice you haven't killed her yet,' said Raphael.

'Thank you very much,' said Evie. 'I am here, you know.'

'I'm just wondering why.' Raphael cast a glance in her direction, but she might just as well have not been there. 'I know you've tried to get others to do it for you, Dolph, yet here she is, exactly where you didn't want her to be.'

'She's where you wanted her to be, though; isn't she, Raphael? You've done a good job on her, judging by the look in her eyes when you arrived.'

'I know why you haven't killed her,' said Raphael, ignoring Dolph's taunting words. 'Because now she's here, you have no way of knowing if that's part of the prophecy.'

'Or yours.'

'I'm ready for it.' Raphael put his hand in his pocket and took out Evie's gun. She guessed without being told that it was already loaded with the silver bullets. Judging by the look on Dolph's face, he knew it too. 'But are you?' Raphael pointed the gun at Dolph.

'You may be able to kill me, but can you kill yourself, Raphael? That's the only way this really ends.'

'He's the alpha . . . ' Evie said to no one in particular. 'Raphael? Is that true? Are you the alpha?'

'I am.'

'But how? Why?'

'He did it to get back at our father for not loving him,' said Dolph.

'My father,' Raphael snapped. 'But it was what you wanted, Dolph. What you always wanted. You see, Evie, Dolph hated that he wasn't born into the Lyell family so that he could share in the curse. Like your brother, he brooded over it for years and years. Then, one night — it was a full moon — he got drunk and kept goading me to bite him. I ignored him at first. I'd made a vow never to bite another human being, and I learned how not to transform during the full moon. It was the only way I could hope for redemption. But he kept on and on, telling me how my father always loved him but never me. How I was the unwanted one whilst he'd been cherished. So I gave him what he wanted. I bit him. And now I'm as damned as he is.'

Raphael looked around the camp at the various witches, vampires and shapeshifters. 'The rest of you can leave. This really doesn't concern you. She is no threat to your way of life. Dolph has only spread that rumour in the hopes that one of you would kill her for him before she got here. Isn't that right, Dolph?'

Dolph nodded reluctantly. There was a lot of murmuring and complaining amongst the other supernaturals, but they packed up their things and left.

Evie looked up at the sky. The moon would rise very soon. The wolf men left behind would begin to change; and whilst part of her was fascinated by the process, the sensible part of her knew that it would be the worst possible place to be.

'The rest of you can go too,' Raphael said to the remaining wolf men. He pointed the gun at them one at a time, and it sent them scattering in all directions. That they recognised Raphael as the alpha was without doubt. None of them were willing to stay and argue with him.

The only ones left in the snow filled forest clearing were Raphael, Evie, Phelan and Dolph.

'Raphael, Dolph,' said Evie. 'This is ridiculous, I have no powers. No way of harming either of you. So why don't we all just leave?'

'Like I said, brother,' said Dolph, 'you did a good job on her. It was clever, getting her to fall in love with you, so that she wouldn't want to hurt you.'

'What?' Evie felt as if the blood ran from her body. She remembered Raphael's passionate lovemaking. Had it all been intended to make her love him? It explained his apparent distaste the first few times he had kissed her.

Raphael walked over to where Evie sat and pulled her to her feet. 'There,' he said, putting the gun into her hand. 'It's loaded with silver bullets.' He put the barrel up against his chest. 'Shoot me directly in the heart and it will all be over.'

'Raphael . . . '

'Go on, do it! My brother might have dreaded this moment, but I haven't. I want it to be over, Evie, and if you're the one who's meant to do it, so be it.'

'Raphael, I can't.'

'Why not? Everything he said was true. Think about it. I knew all the time that I was the one you were really looking for, and I hid that from you. I did it long enough to make you fall in love with me. You don't think I really wanted to kiss you, did you?' When he curled his lips in distaste, he might just as well have shot Evie in the heart. 'For pity's sake, just pull the trigger and have done with it.'

Evie felt a flash of anger, and her finger tightened on the trigger. She could easily kill him for what he had done to her. He had betrayed her, only keeping her close to protect his own skin. It depended just how much of her great-great-grandmother was in her.

She glanced up momentarily and saw that the moon was on the rise. She began to think about everything she had been told in the past few days. It occurred to her that for a curse to work, not only does the person being cursed have to believe it, but the one doing the curse has to believe it, too. If the Shaman did not believe he could kill someone just by pointing a finger at them, then it would not be credible to the one he cursed. Could she believe enough for it to work? She had no powers. She was not her great-great-grandmother. But she did have something that everyone else around her seemed to have lost. She had faith.

'It's Christmas Day,' she whispered.

'I'm aware of that,' said Raphael. 'And there's a full moon, and you're exactly where you're supposed to be, bringing an end to all this. Just do it, Evie.'

'Do you remember Christmases at home, Phelan?' she asked, ignoring Raphael.

'Yes.'

'It was the only time we were really happy. Do you remember? Even Papa was happy, because at Christmas everyone believes in God, even those who lack faith the rest of the year. Do you ever wonder why we celebrate the birth of His son, and then months later celebrate His death?'

'I can't say I do,' said Dolph, sighing. But his eyes were fixed on the gun pointing at Raphael's chest.

'Jesus was born to die for our sins. Think about what that means for a moment. What it means is that God was saying to us that it's alright to make mistakes. It's alright to be human and fallible. As long as we learn from those mistakes. He will forgive us. But I think He was also saying that we sometimes have to forgive ourselves, too, and not be haunted by the things we have done.'

Evie lowered the gun, and switched hands. She put her right hand on Raphael's chest. She could feel his heart beating rapidly. The sudden gasp from his chest suggested that he was having problems controlling himself. Any moment now he would begin to change into a werewolf, closely followed by Dolph. She had to get the words right, she knew that, but her closeness to Raphael and the pain she felt in knowing he did not love her constricted her throat. She took a deep breath.

'One thing you've always said is that demons are still human beings. You argued to save them when I was ready to kill them. So you understand that others can make mistakes, yet you can't forgive yourself for yours.' Evie took a deep breath. 'What my great-great-grandmother did was wrong. Yes, she had been hurt and deceived, but no one has the right to demand love from another, and she had no right to make their children suffer too. This is why I am not going to demand love from you, Raphael. I have no right to do so. I forgive you for misleading me.'

'Evie . . .'

'No, wait — I have to say this, and say it quickly. I forgive you for misleading me, but more importantly I think you should forgive yourself for what you did to Dolph. You made a mistake, that's all. Whether you care about me or not, you do care about others, and you help those whom you know are good people, so I know there's goodness in you. I am not my great-great-grandmother, and I am certainly not a witch; but if it is within my power at all, then, because I love you, I lift the curse that has afflicted your family.'

'No!' Dolph exclaimed.

'I set you free from the curse, Raphael, and in doing so, I set Dolph free.'

What happened next was a blur. Evie felt the gun snatched from her hand, before the cold barrel touched her temple. Before Raphael could react and knock his stepbrother down, Phelan launched himself across the clearing. The next moment she saw her brother and Dolph grappling on the ground. Two shots rang out, one after the other.

Evie ran over to her brother, and cradled him in her arms.

'No, Phelan, no.' Tears sprung from her eyes. Her brother had sacrificed himself to save her.

'Tell Papa I'm sorry,' he whispered. 'And that I wish I could have come home.' He reached up and stroked his sister's face. 'You really are the clever one,' he said. 'You've set us all free.'

'Phelan was never afflicted with Lycanthropy, Papa,' Evie told her father. They sat at the window in the hotel room in Budapest, with all their bags packed ready to leave on the evening train. 'He had consumption, and could not bear to let you know for fear of causing you pain. But I want you to know he died without suffering, and with your name on his lips. He said to say he was sorry.'

The reverend gazed out of the window, his old eyes damp with unshed tears. 'He was sorry? I am the one who should be sorry. I made a mess of things, Evie.' Evie looked up in surprise. Her father had never called her Evie before. 'I did not know how to be a father, perhaps because my father did not know how to be one.'

'I think you should forgive yourself for your mistakes, Papa.'

'I don't know if I can, child. They have cost too much. I did love your mother, you know. More than I ever loved anyone in my life. I did not know how to express it. I only hope that she now knows what's in my heart. I hope Phelan knows it too.' He reached across and took Evie's hand. 'I am not going to make the same mistake with you, child. I want you to know now how much your father loves you, and how proud I am of you and all that you've done. I've been thinking. They're letting young women into universities nowadays. When we get back to England, why don't we look into it and see if we can find you a place?'

'I . . . I don't know what I want to do, Papa. I don't want to leave you.'

'You must. I will be perfectly able to cope. I'll have Polly to take care of me.'

'Papa . . . I . . . ' Evie swallowed hard.

'Tell me about it, child.'

'I don't know if I dare.'

'A moment ago, you told me to forgive myself. Now I ask you to do the same.'

So Evie told him about Raphael. Not

everything. She left out the parts about the vampires and the shapeshifters. Her father's world had been rocked enough without adding more confusion, or by worrying him that she had been afflicted with a mental illness. She did tell him about what happened in the forest, but kept up the pretence that both Raphael and Dolph were suffering from the mental affliction, and that she had lifted the curse using the power of the mind — and of God — rather than the supernatural. She did not tell him how her brother had really died, because she knew that would be too painful to hear. 'I love Raphael,' she said when her story had ended. 'But he does not love me.'

'Then he's a fool,' said the reverend.

'Thank you for that, Papa.' Evie smiled through her tears.

'And after what you told me, I really wonder that you don't study theology. You're rather good at it, by the sound of things. You understand humanity better than I ever have.'

'I think,' Evie said thoughtfully, 'that sometimes you have to see people behave inhumanly to understand humanity.' She did not elaborate and her father did not ask her to. She suspected that he preferred not to. He must realise she had left things out of her story, but he did not press her for more information.

Just before they left, Evie took a last walk around Budapest. She did not know if she always intended to turn up at Raphael's office, or whether it was just chance. But she found it locked up. The old groom told her that Professor Raphael had gone away, and he did not know when he would return.

She had not seen him since Christmas night. They had buried Phelan and Dolph in the forest, then rode back to the nearest train station. He had said very little to her. When she got on the train, she looked around to see if he followed, but instead he stood on the platform and watched her leave without a word.

She had cried all the way back to

Budapest. Parting from him was the best thing, she knew that. She could not bear for him to pretend he loved her out of gratitude. Assuming that was what he felt. Perhaps he was as angry with her as Dolph had been. It was one thing to think of having a curse lifted, but quite another to have lost it along with the powers that went with it. He might well resent her.

But what if it had not worked? What if he had only managed to control himself long enough to let her think it had? He had said that he was able to stop the demon from appearing on the full moon. He had many years of practice in doing so.

He was not superstitious in the way Dolph had been. Raphael knew all the tricks and how they worked on the mind. In which case, he had no need of ensuring Evie's affections anymore. Perhaps he was with Alexia, laughing over the stupid girl he had fooled into loving him.

It was with a sense of regret that Evie

got onto the train with her father later that evening. How could she love this region so much when it held so much darkness? All she knew was that she had never had so much excitement, or felt so much heartache — in fact, felt so human and alive — until she had arrived there.

14

'Is your Papa well?' asked Natalia. She and Evie sat in a café in Bucharest, drinking strong, sweet black coffee. Evie had looked up her old friend from the train as soon as she arrived several months earlier. Christmas was coming again, and outside the streets were decorated ready for the festivities.

Evie put down her letter. 'Yes, he's having a wonderful time in the Holy Land. He says the people are warm and welcoming and he's enjoying learning about different faiths. He also said Polly keeps moaning about the heat and the flies, but he thinks she secretly loves being amongst what she calls 'the infidel'. Polly is convinced that anyone who isn't British and a Christian is involved in all sorts of nefarious night-time practices. If only she could get them to tell her all the details so she could be truly horrified. She'd be really disappointed to learn that, like most of us, they go home at night, eat their dinner, read a good book then go to bed only to sleep.'

Natalia laughed. 'And you, my friend. Are you well? Your Hungarian is coming along nicely.'

'I'm fine, Natalia. I love it at the university.' Unable to find any of the courses she wanted in British universities, Evie had taken the decision to move to Romania, where a Professor at the university was willing to let her study myths and legends. 'What about you? How is young Vitali?'

'He is a handful, as ever. He misses his Papa. Sometimes I feel sorry for these young children who have governesses, even if it means I would be out of a job if they did not. I love him, but it is not the same as his own blood.'

'No, I understand that.' Evie instinctively thought of another little boy starved of his father's love. She pushed the thought aside. She had almost forgotten Raphael. Or, at least, that was what she told herself during the five minutes of the day she managed not to remember him.

'You still think of him?'

'No. Not much.' Evie smiled. Natalia was the only person she had ever been able to tell the whole story to. For a long time she had tried to convince herself that it was a dream, or that she had imagined it. One day, she might convince herself, but not yet. 'Only every other minute. I've never met anyone like him, Natalia, and I don't think I shall again.'

'What about that young man at the university who is paying you attention?'

'Oh, him; he's alright, I suppose. He's nice to have as a friend. But I don't have any romantic feelings towards him.'

As Evie spoke, the proprietor of the café came from behind the counter to shoo a dog out of the door. Evie glanced over idly, and saw that the dog was big and black. No, it could not be . . .

'Sergei,' she said. She got up, and the dog gave one sharp bark before running out into the street. 'Sergei!' she called, running after him. 'Sergei, is that you? Please don't run away. I am not angry with you.' She turned around and called back to her friend. 'Natalia, please settle the bill. I'll pay you back later.'

She followed the dog through the streets of Bucharest, and began to think she might have got it wrong. It was just a dog, probably a stray looking for food. But whenever she stopped, the dog stopped too, and barked at her.

'You could just change, you know,' she said, when she had run so far she had a stitch in her side. 'So I know it's definitely you.'

The dog led her down an alleyway, and for the first time it occurred to her that it might be a trap. Sergei had betrayed her before. But that was when Dolph saw her as a threat. Dolph was dead, and as far as Evie knew she was no threat to anyone.

She was too curious to turn back. She wanted to know where the dog was leading her. He took her through the alley to an inner courtyard, and then through the door of one of the buildings and up a flight of stairs. Finally, at the top of the staircase, in front of an open door, the dog became Sergei, looming at the top of the staircase. 'I found her,' he said. 'I bring her to you, just as you asked.'

'Bring me to who?' asked Evie. 'What's going on, Sergei?' She climbed the stairs, even though all her instincts told her she should run away.

A figure appeared in the open doorway. 'Hello, Evie. I went all the way to England looking for you, only to find out you were right here, on my doorstep.'

'Raphael . . . ' Her heart skipped a beat to see him standing in front of her. He looked different. Tidier and more respectable. His hair was shorter, he had shaved off his beard, and he wore a good suit.

Sergei smiled. 'Now you are reunited, I will go.' He passed Evie on the landing. 'I hope I am forgiven for what I did last year, Evangeline.'

She took the big Cossack's hands in hers and kissed both his cheeks. 'Of course you are, Sergei. Is Tasha safe and well?'

'She is very safe, thank you. I must go now.'

Evie and Raphael were left alone, looking at each other, neither knowing what to say.

'You . . . '

'You . . . '

'No, you first,' said Raphael.

'I was just thinking that you look very tidy.'

'Well, thanks to you, I have to be respectable now. No more tearing around the countryside looking like a tramp.'

'You're angry with me . . . '

'No, Evie. I'm grateful, really I am. I want to show you something. Will you take a trip with me?'

'Where?'

'You'll see when we get there. Unless you're tired of adventure.' The twinkle in his eyes showed that there was still some of the old Raphael there. He might say he was respectable, but Evie suspected it was only an act; for what reason, though, she did not know.

'Alright, I'll come with you.'

'Your hair has grown back,' he said, as they rode on a sleigh through the streets of Bucharest. 'I rather liked it short.'

'You said you liked it long.'

'Did I? Well, perhaps both suit you.'

It was difficult to say much more with the icy wind in their faces. They had to cover up well with fur and scarves around their mouths. He took them out of the city, and into the countryside. A couple of hours later, they came to a clearing in a forest.

'The cottage!' said Evie. 'You've built on to it.' What had been a building with two large rooms had spread through the clearing, turning it into a double-fronted house, with extra rooms upstairs.

'Yes, I've been working on it for a while. Come on, I'll give you the tour. You may want to change some furnishings, but that's fine by me. I just wanted it ready for when you arrived.'

Evie tried not to think of the implications of what he had just said, in case she had got it terribly wrong. And if he did mean that, why would he not simply say it?

He had added a dining room, a sitting room and a small study to the cottage downstairs. Upstairs there were three bedrooms and a bathroom. He had chosen the furnishings well, though Evie blushed when she saw that one of the smaller bedrooms had a cradle.

'You're getting married,' she said, trying to hide her emotions. 'That's why you're all dressed up and tidy.'

'That was the general idea, yes.'

'I see. I'm very happy for you, Raphael. Really, I am. I hope you and your wife will be very happy together.'

'I hope so, too.'

Evie could not bear it any longer. She

turned and ran down the stairs. 'I really should be getting back,' she said, her voice full of false cheer. 'I have lectures to attend in the morning, and my Professor doesn't like it if I'm late, and . . . '

Raphael followed her down the stairs, and caught her by the arm. 'Evie, I'd hoped you would stay. I mean, there are two bedrooms now, so we don't have to take shifts; and then when we marry . . . '

'When we marry? What do you mean?'

'That's why I brought you here.' He ran his fingers through his hair. 'I've got it all wrong. I intended to cook dinner for you, and then propose in a romantic way.'

'But I haven't seen you for nearly a year. You just let me leave.'

'I know. I can explain that. You see, I didn't know what would happen when the curse was lifted. That was, *if* it had been lifted. For all I knew, I might have even died of old age within a few weeks. I didn't think it was fair to ask you to stay under those circumstances. So I came back here until I was sure what would happen. Whilst I was here, I rebuilt the place. That was when I realised what a gift you had given me. You gave me the chance to be human, Evie, and the chance to live a normal life and eventually grow old.'

'And now you're grateful.'

'Of course I'm grateful. It was the best Christmas gift I could have ever had.'

'Raphael, you don't have to marry me because you're grateful.'

'That's not the only reason. I love you.'

'No, you don't! You said you didn't. Or, if you do, it's only out of gratitude.'

'How dare you tell me what I feel, Evie?'

'I'm only telling you what you told me.'

'And you believed all that, did you?'

'Well, yes; why would I not?'

Raphael sighed. 'No, you're right. Why would you not believe it? Don't you ever wonder why I left you at the crystal palace?'

'You'd had enough of me. Or you'd succeeded in making me fall in love with you. Maybe a bit of both.'

'I left you because for the first time in many years I felt myself losing control. I came very close to it. I was terrified that when the full moon came, I would change and hurt you. I couldn't bear the thought of that. So I had to go. But I came back and you'd gone. I saw there were sets of hooves leading to the palace, so I followed their trail to you. I realised that destiny had indeed decided you and I should be in that forest on that night. I do love you, Evie.'

'Enough? Is that it? You love me just enough, because you're grateful to me? I'm sorry, but I don't think I can accept that as a basis for marriage.' And yet Evie knew that if Raphael argued with her for just a little while longer, she would accept him. It was better than the pain of losing him again.

Raphael laughed. 'You never knew what your great-great-grandmother's dream was about, did you?'

'Yes, she said that someone of her blood would come along and change things for the supernaturals, bringing an end to their way of life. Or something like that.' Evie had heard so many different stories, it was hard to know which were correct.

'No, she dreamed that one day someone of her blood would fall in love with someone of my blood, and when that love was returned unconditionally the curse would be broken.'

'What?'

Raphael pulled her into his arms. 'I don't just love you enough, Evie. I love you more than enough. I love you until I lose all control, and I can't think of anyone but you. Why do you think I wanted to kill Vladimir? How dare he kiss you when it should only be me kissing you?'

'But he looked like you. I don't know how, but somehow he did. When I said

'I love you', I thought I was saying it to you.'

Raphael smiled. He really did have the most wonderful smile. 'I realised how stupid I'd been when it was too late. I'm sorry I made you feel the way you did. Will you forgive me?'

Evie rested her head on his chest. 'I am a bit disappointed.'

'Why, darling? Don't you like the cottage?'

'Oh, I love the cottage; and I love you, Raphael. But I thought all the things I said in the forest on Christmas Day made a real difference.'

'They did make a difference. It was only then that I realised how much I really do love you. I had been denying it to myself for fear of harming you if I lost control. Your words set me free, not just from the spell but also from my own fears.' He stroked her hair. 'Last year, you gave me the most wonderful gift I have ever received. Will you give me another gift this year, darling?'

'Of course. What do you want?' She

prayed that the answer would be the one she had longed to hear.

'Will you be my wife?'

Evie reached up and kissed him until neither of them could breathe. For the first time she was able to show him all the love she had suppressed, and it seemed to her that Raphael no longer held his kisses in check. He pulled back his head and laughed. 'I'm not entirely convinced you're not a witch,' he said, rocking her playfully in his arms. 'But if you are, don't go promising that some great-great-granddaughter in the future might undo the curse. I think it can only be a blessing if *our* children and grandchildren live under this spell for all eternity.'

'Then, with all the powers at my disposal, consider yourself truly blessed,' said Evie, kissing him again.

We do hope that you have enjoyed reading this large print book.

Did you know that all of our titles are available for purchase?

We publish a wide range of high quality large print books including:
Romances, Mysteries, Classics
General Fiction
Non Fiction and Westerns

Special interest titles available in large print are:
The Little Oxford Dictionary
Music Book, Song Book
Hymn Book, Service Book

Also available from us courtesy of Oxford University Press:
Young Readers' Dictionary
(large print edition)
Young Readers' Thesaurus
(large print edition)

For further information or a free brochure, please contact us at:
Ulverscroft Large Print Books Ltd.,
The Green, Bradgate Road, Anstey,
Leicester, LE7 7FU, England.
Tel: (00 44) **0116 236 4325**
Fax: (00 44) **0116 234 0205**

Other titles in the
Linford Romance Library:

INTRIGUE IN ROME

Phyllis Mallett

Gail Bennett's working holiday in Rome takes an unexpectedly sinister turn as soon as she arrives at her hotel. Why does the receptionist give out her personal details to someone on the phone? Who is the mysterious man she spies checking her car over? Soon she meets Paul, a handsome Englishman keen to romance her — but he is not what he seems. And how does Donato — Italian, charming — fit into the picture? Gail knows that one of them can save her, while the other could be the death of her . . .

THE FAMILY AT CLOCKMAKERS COTTAGE

June Davies

Feeling bereft after her sister Fanny gets married and moves away, young Amy Macfarlene must manage Clockmakers Cottage on her own, while earning a living as a parlour maid and seamstress for a wealthy local family, the Paslews. Her wayward brother Rory is a constant concern, as he is clearly embroiled in some shady dealings and refuses all offers of help. Amy's childhood sweetheart Dan is a comfort to her — but as her friendship with the handsome Gilbert Paslew grows, so do her uncertainties about her future . . .

RACHEL'S FLOWERS

Christina Green

Rachel Swann takes a sabbatical from her London floristry job to come home and temporarily manage the family plant nursery. But then it emerges that her uncle has also asked the globetrotting plant collector Benjamin Hunter to do the self-same task! Wary of Ben's exotic plans for the establishment, Rachel is determined to keep the nursery running in its traditional manner. But as the two work together, they cannot ignore the seeds of a special relationship slowly blooming between them . . .

UNEASY ALLIANCE

Wendy Kremer

Joanne is intelligent, capable — and beautiful. Her female colleagues always assume this plays a major part in her rapid promotions, no matter where she works, and now all she has to show for her efforts is her current state of unemployment and a string of short-lived jobs on her CV. Signing up with an exclusive dating agency, she meets tycoon Benedict North — an exceptional, charismatic man. But when she finally lands a job, Joanne is unsure of whether there is room in her life for him — despite her growing feelings . . .